MURDERERS' ROW

DONALD HAMILTON

A *MATT HELM* NOVEL

MURDERERS' ROW

TITAN BOOKS

Murderers' Row
Print edition ISBN: 9780857683403
E-book edition ISBN: 9781781162347

Published by Titan Books
A division of Titan Publishing Group Ltd
144 Southwark Street, London SE1 0UP

First edition: August 2013
1 2 3 4 5 6 7 8 9 10

A CIP catalogue record for this title is available from the British Library.

Printed and bound in the United States.

Did you enjoy this book? We love to hear from our readers.
Please email us at readerfeedback@titanemail.com or write to us at
Reader Feedback at the above address.

To receive advance information, news, competitions, and exclusive
offers online, please sign up for the Titan newsletter on our website:
www.titanbooks.com

MURDERERS' ROW

1

The motel was on the left side of the highway leading from Washington, D.C., to the eastern shore of Maryland by way of the Chesapeake Bay Bridge. So said the map; I'd never been there and wasn't about to go. At least I didn't think I was. In my line of business, you can't ever be absolutely sure where you'll wind up tomorrow.

As I made the turn and headed into the driveway, my watch said I was arriving precisely on schedule at a quarter-past-ten in the evening. I parked the little car that had been assigned to me among others displaying an assortment of license plates. Mine read Illinois, and I had a complete and phony identity to go with it, in case of trouble.

My real name is Helm—Matthew Helm—and certain government records have me cross-filed under the code name Eric, but for the evening I was James A. Peters, employed by Atlas Enterprises, Inc., a Chicago firm. The nature of the company, and my exact position with them, remained carefully unspecified on the identification I carried. Anyone who became really interested, however— interested enough, say, to send a set of fingerprints to the Chicago police—would be informed that I was known locally as Jimmy (the Lash) Petroni, a man with influential friends and an unsavory reputation.

In other words, I wasn't, for the record, a very nice guy. It was just as well. The job wasn't a very nice job. In fact, one agent had already turned it down.

"Sentimentality!" Mac had snorted, in his Washington office on the second floor of a rather ancient building, never mind where. "These delicate buds we get nowadays, nurtured on beautiful thoughts of peace, security, and social adjustment! They may be brave and patriotic enough in the right situations, but the thought of violence turns them inside out. Not one of them would kill a fly, I sometimes think, to save an entire nation from dying of yellow fever."

"Yes, sir," I said. "Yellow fever isn't carried by flies, sir. It's transmitted by mosquitoes."

"Indeed?" he said. "That's very interesting. I could have made it an order, but the young fool probably would have botched the job, feeling the way he did. It's a damn nuisance. Being on the spot, he was the logical person. However, I remembered that you were on your way in from Cuba; and I thought you might like to spend a little time by the seashore—the bay shore, to be exact. Not that you'll have much time for swimming, if everything goes according to plan."

"I'm a lousy swimmer, anyway," I said. "I lack buoyancy, or something. Besides, it's getting a little late in the season."

"You know the area. You took two weeks of small boat training at Annapolis during the war, according to the files."

"Yes, sir, but there wasn't much time for sight-seeing. I wouldn't say I'd learned much about the area. Besides, it will have changed considerably since those days." Subtlety wasn't getting me anywhere, so I said bluntly, "Besides, there was some talk of a month's leave, sir."

"I'm sorry about that," he said smoothly. "However, we are setting a trap. We can't risk failure because a sentimental boy hasn't got the stomach to prepare the bait properly."

"No, sir."

"I hope I'm not interfering with any plans of long standing."

"No, sir," I said dryly. "It was only arranged some six months ago—subject, of course, to the call of duty. I was only on my way to Texas to see a lady."

"I see." His voice was cool. "That one."

"You don't approve, sir? She helped us out once."

"Against her will," he said. "Very much against her will, as I recall. She is rich, irresponsible, jealous, impulsive, and totally unreliable, Eric."

The indictment gave him away. The whole thing was beginning to make sense. I was being recalled from leave to keep me from getting further involved with a woman he considered unsuitable, as a rich college boy might be sent on a sea voyage to forget a pretty waitress. I tried not to show anger. It would be easy enough to blurt out that my private life was none of his damn business, but it wouldn't be true. In our line of work, there's no such thing as a private life.

I said carefully, "Gail Hendricks is all right, sir. She's seen us at work and she knows the score. I don't have to pretend to be a respectable car salesman, or something, when I'm with her. And she doesn't have to pretend to be a fragile and sensitive southern beauty, either. I happen to know—and she knows I know—that she's just about as fragile and sensitive as a female lynx. It makes for a beautiful relationship, sir. I hope you aren't going to ask me to give it up."

It was obviously what he'd had in mind, but the direct question, and the implied submissiveness, put him off balance, as I'd hoped it would.

"No," he said quickly, "no, of course not, but I will have to ask you to postpone your trip West until you've attended to this matter. It is quite important, and it shouldn't delay you more than a few days."

"Yes, sir."

"Now go see Dr. Perry. I don't want to waste time briefing you further until you know exactly what's involved."

I had seen Dr. Perry, a cheerfully callous young medical man in a starched white coat. I'd been briefed, and now I got out of the car and walked past the motel swimming pool, which was empty. A breeze carrying a hint of autumn dipped over the windbreak on the far side and ruffled the surface. The submerged lights made the water look blue-green, luminous, and very cold, like the pool at the foot of a mountain glacier. I didn't have the slightest desire to try it out.

Some tourists drove up to the office, at the other end of the motel, where there was also a cocktail lounge, coffee shop, and dining room. You can still tell them from hotels, however. Hotels have elevators. The newcomers paid no attention to me, as I let myself into the unit with the right number, using the key Mac had given me.

"Jean has been one of our best female operatives," he'd said, pushing the key across the desk to me. "Very good appearance, attractive without being conspicuous, the pleasant young suburban-matron type. It's most unfortunate. We do encounter such breakdowns now and then, you know; and alcoholism is almost always one of the symptoms. Have you noticed how these slightly plump, pretty, smooth-faced women seem to crack up more readily than any other kind?"

"No, sir," I said. "I hadn't noticed."

"It's a fact," he said. "That, of course, is why she was selected for the assignment originally. She could make it believable, if anyone could. When the matter suddenly became urgent…" He paused, and let that line of thought go. "As I said, she is good. In addition to drinking too much, she has been showing convincing signs of disaffection, not to say, you understand, of active disloyalty. Overtures have been made. It is very distressing. We are very much

disturbed." He looked at me across the big desk. The
window behind him made his expression difficult to read.
"At least that is the impression we are trying to convey—
trying very hard to convey. Do I make myself clear?"

"Yes, sir," I said. "It's clear."

It was still clear as I entered the room and closed the
door behind me. I didn't have to worry about fingerprints,
since I was wearing gloves. They made me feel like a
hardened criminal. All the lights in the place were on.
There was the usual blond motel-modern furniture.
There was also as much of a mess as one female lush
could make without really straining herself, in a room
that had presumably been cleaned by the management
earlier in the day.

There was a full fifth of whisky on the dresser, and
a half-empty one standing beside a soiled glass on the
telephone stand by the big double bed, which was rumpled
as if she'd taken an afternoon nap—or just passed out
temporarily—on top of the covers. A stocking with a run
in it had been discarded on the floor by the wastebasket,
a near miss, I guess.

Other garments of an intimate nature, some flimsy,
some surprisingly sturdy, were distributed about the
premises, again mostly on the floor, along with some wads
of Kleenex, the afternoon paper, a pair of thong sandals,
a fuzzy pink sweater, and a pair of pink corduroy pants,
the narrow, tapered style all women seem to have adopted
lately, whether it suits their rear ends or not. Female rears
being what they are, mostly it doesn't.

I'm strictly an anti-pants man myself, where women are concerned, but with all the mad trousers you see on the street nowadays, it's getting so even jeans look good, while a well-cut pair of Bermuda shorts is a real treat.

I sat down to wait in the big chair facing the TV set, which was turned off. I didn't bother to look around for mikes or wires. Mac had said there'd be some, and that the phone was probably tapped as well, which figured. If the opposition was interested in our supposedly drunk and disloyal operative at all, they'd be checking up to see if she were the real thing or a plant.

I hadn't the slightest intention of interfering with any of their electronic equipment. In fact, I hoped it was all in first-class condition and working well, since it was my job to make Jean's act more plausible, and I wanted an audience.

2

"Plausible,' I'd said in Washington. "Yes, sir. Just how plausible can you get? Does this lady know what she's let herself in for?"

"She knows," Mac said. "That is, she doesn't know the details; she preferred not to hear them, which was only natural. But she knows that it will hurt, and that she won't be pretty to look at for a couple of weeks. Certainly she has been consulted. She has agreed." He frowned at me across the desk. "There are two things for you to keep in mind. She has to survive, of course. She even has to be able to function after a fashion within a reasonable time, say three or four days. On the other hand, it must be convincing. Just a dramatic black eye and some spectacularly damaged clothing won't buy her a thing except a ticket to the bottom of the Bay."

"I see," I said. "Do I get to know what it's all about, sir, or would you prefer to keep me ignorant."

"A man slipped through our fingers down there, last

year," Mac said. "We'd been after him for a long time; he was high on the removal list. He was finally spotted right here in Washington. There was no real error made, but as you know, for diplomatic reasons we do not operate within certain zones, of which metropolitan Washington is one. It is preferred that we take no action within twenty-five miles of the city." He grimaced. "It is a reasonable requirement, I suppose, but the people who set these limits often have no idea what their regulations mean to the people who have to do the work."

"No, sir."

"When the subject finally departed from Washington, he made for Annapolis. From there, he soon disappeared, leaving behind our agent, dead."

I raised my eyebrows. "No error, you say, sir? Getting killed is a serious mistake, in my book."

Mac shrugged. "I'll grant that, but Ames was a good operative, and he had reason to believe he was dealing with one man only. Apparently he ran into something bigger down near Chesapeake Bay."

"Ames?" I said. "I worked with him in California, a couple of jobs back."

"I know." Mac did not look up. "That is another reason I thought you might like to help out with this business, even if it means postponing your date in Texas."

I laughed shortly. "You're an optimist, sir. Some things don't postpone very well. Gail is not the patient type. As for Ames, he was one of those portable-radio jerks. I came close to making him eat the thing, one transistor at a time. Goddamn a man who'll climb an eight-thousand-foot mountain just to turn on that kind of noise. On the other hand, I'll hand it to him, he did fry a mean flapjack, and he had a way with fresh-caught trout—" I stopped. After a moment, I said, "They got him from behind, didn't they?"

"Yes. He was found on a beach with a broken neck. Apparently somebody slipped up on him while he was stalking the subject. How did you know?"

"He would get excited and forget to watch his back. It never seemed to occur to him that somebody might be stalking *him*. I warned him. Ah, hell. Scratch Ames, a good man with a skillet."

"Yes," Mac said. "As I was saying, after the killing, the subject disappeared completely. Some months later, he was reported in Europe, although he had not been seen leaving the country by any of the usual channels."

"Who was it?"

"His name doesn't matter," Mac said. "One of our people took care of him over there. I checked with other departments, and found that this wasn't the first mysterious disappearance from that neighborhood. They suspect the existence of a cell or organization with a way station, a cooling-off place, somewhere along the Bay, where fugitives can be hidden indefinitely until transportation is ready for them. Ships move up and down the Bay all the time, remember: big, ocean-going ships. In theory, they can be stopped and searched until they pass the Chesapeake Capes, at the mouth of the Bay, and get three miles out to sea. In practice, searching a ship of any size, under way, is an awkward proposition."

I said, "According to what I recall from my brief association with the U.S. Navy, Chesapeake Bay is some two hundred miles long and up to twenty miles wide. The map shows rivers, swamps, bays, inlets, islands—"

"The nautical term is chart."

"Excuse me, sir. Chart."

"Your point is well taken, however," Mac said. "With our limited facilities, it would be fruitless to try to search such an area for a camouflaged waterfront hideout. And we don't even know that it's on the water, although everything indicates that the pickups are made by boat, and it seems likely that the deliveries are made the same way. But in any case, it's a job well beyond our resources, which is why we approached the problem from a slightly different angle."

"I thought we were supposed to be specialists of a sort, sir. What's the matter with all the bright government boys with college degrees and button-down collars—the clean-cut lads who can teach judo to the Japanese and shoot a silhouette target to shreds in three-fifths of a second, starting with their hands tied behind them? Can't they manage to find this subversives' bus stop by themselves?"

Mac looked up. "You're forgetting Ames," he said.

"You said the man he was after had been taken care of."

"To be sure." Mac's voice was cold. "There are, however, some people in the neighborhood of Annapolis, not forty miles from here, who share in the responsibility.

An organization like ours cannot afford to overlook interference, particularly when it results in the death of one of our people. That is why I asked that the job be assigned to us." He made a little face. "The others were glad to let us have it. Apparently there are some local political considerations that make it awkward to handle. You might keep that in mind."

"Yes, sir," I said. "So our objective is really teaching these outsiders to be careful who they bump off."

"Let us say," Mac said carefully, "they must learn not to monkey with the buzz saw when it is busy cutting wood."

There was a silence. I looked past him, out the bright window and could see one of the shining white buildings in which earnest men conduct the nation's business openly, with reporters in attendance. I thought about how nice it would be if it could all be handled like that.

I said, "Yes, sir. So we are throwing this agent of ours, Jean, down the rathole to see where she comes out. If she comes out. What makes you think they'll fall for her alcoholic act, sir?"

"That is your job, to make them fall for it," he said. "Don't forget, they will want to fall for it. They do not normally get any of our senior people alive and willing to talk. They'd like to know more about us. There's still a body of official opinion over there to the effect that no decadent democratic society could possibly support a tough agency like ours; that we're a fiction invented by our opposite numbers over there to excuse their failures. There are people over there who would be very glad to have an agent of ours put on exhibit. I think they will take the bait if it is properly presented."

I nodded. "And suppose they do accept Jean for what she claims to be, a potential deserter, what then?"

"Her original orders were to identify the route and the lay-over station, as well as the people involved, as far as possible. Then she was to extricate herself by any available means, and report. No other action was required of her."

"I'd say it was plenty, sir."

"Yes. Unfortunately, I have had to modify those orders in the light of new information." He hesitated, then he drew a piece of paper towards him, took the ball-point desk pen out of its holder and printed a single word. He replaced the pen and pushed the paper across the desk towards me, turning it so that I could read what he had written. "Do you know what that word means, Eric?"

I looked at the paper. The word, printed in capital letters, was AUDAP. It meant nothing to me. "No, sir. They play so many games with the alphabet around here, I've given up trying to figure them out."

Mac took back the piece of paper and drew an ash-stand closer. He burned the paper carefully, powdered the ashes, and tripped the trap to let them fall into the base of the stand.

"That word," he said, "represents one of the most highly classified secrets in Washington, and you've never seen it, of course."

"Of course."

"It's very, very secret," he said. "Only we and the Russians know about it, nobody else."

"I see."

"They do not, however, know as much as they would like. Do you know anything about submarines, Eric?"

"Yes, sir. They travel under water."

"Until recently this was not strictly true," Mac said. "Until recently, a submarine was a surface vessel capable of submerging for short periods of time. Even so, it was a potent naval weapon. Why?"

"I suppose, because when it's submerged, you can't see it."

"Precisely. And with the advent of, first the snorkel, and then nuclear power, enabling the boats to go under water and stay there,his advantage has increased tremendously. Radar doesn't work under water. Sonar is relatively short range and unreliable; besides, the instrument has to be in the water to be effective. This makes it impractical for use from fast search airplanes; the only way large sea areas can be efficiently patrolled." He looked at me across the desk, like a teacher in a classroom. "Do you know which weapon of ours the Russians fear most?"

I shrugged. "The big bombers, I suppose, sir. Or the Atlas missiles with nuclear warheads."

"If they haven't found some kind of an answer to bombers yet, after all the time they've had to work at it, they're not as smart as I think. And the big intercontinental ballistic missiles still have to be fired from fixed sites which can be located by intelligence work—we don't make it very difficult—and more or less neutralized by other missiles or by sabotage. No, the weapon they really fear is the weapon they can't neutralize because they can't find it. It is the weapon we operate out of Holy Loch, Scotland: the Polaris submarine." Mac got up and walked to the window and spoke without looking around. "Of course, what I have told you is the Navy version. An Army or Air Force man might give a different picture. Still, the admiral who explained the situation to me was most persuasive."

"Yes, sir."

"Each Polaris submarine carries sixteen Polaris missiles," Mac said, regarding the sunny view outside. "At present the range is about a thousand miles, but it is being extended. We have—the exact number is confidential—say, half-a-dozen of these submarines operational, but more are being built. Even the half-dozen already on patrol in northern waters give the man in the Kremlin a great deal to think about at night, I should imagine. Six times sixteen is ninety-six nuclear missiles, waiting invisibly under the ocean within range of his major cities. The submarines don't even have to surface to shoot. There's nothing he can do about them—unless he can locate them first." He paused. "The word I wrote down for you, AUDAP, stands for a little gadget just invented known as an Airborne Underwater Detection Apparatus."

There was a short silence. Mac swung from the window and returned to his chair and sat down facing me. He put the tips of his fingers together delicately, and looked at them.

"We don't know," he said, "the mind of the opposition. We don't know how close they are to taking the big gamble. We do know that, even discounting Navy enthusiasm, the Polaris submarine must be a powerful deterrent. But if they should get their hands on a device that gave them some hope of neutralizing that deterrent—" He shrugged expressively.

"Have they?"

"No," Mac said. "The device is safe. The plans are safe. However, the man who invented the device and drew up the plans has disappeared, a gentleman named Dr. Norman Michaelis."

"I see." I frowned thoughtfully. "Was he kidnaped or did he go under his own power?"

"He was on vacation, resting up from his labors on AUDAP. He disappeared while sailing alone on the Bay in a small boat. The wind dropped towards evening, as it does. Some people in a power boat offered him a tow, but he refused it, saying he'd work his way in under sail. Well after dark, the friends with whom he was staying went out in a motor cruiser to see how he was making out. They found the boat sailing merrily along on the evening breeze with no one on board."

"The fact that he refused a tow might indicate something."

"If you don't know sailors," Mac said, "it might. However, a real sailboat man—as Michaelis seems to be—would rather spend all night trying to get home on a whisper of breeze, rather than be snatched into port at the end of a towline."

"I'll take your word for it," I said. "This nautical kick is out of my line."

"The details don't matter, and the question of whether or not Michaelis absconded voluntarily is also quite irrelevant. Whatever he knows, he can be made to tell, you know that. If they once get him over there, and their experts get to work on him with the latest drugs and interrogation techniques, he will talk freely whether he wants to or not. They all do. It must not be allowed to happen. That is why we—you—have to take such drastic means to bring matters to a head where Jean is concerned. We have to sell them on her, very quickly. If we have luck, and Michaelis and she are held for the same shipment— apparently they don't ship very often, which improves our chances. But they have to be persuaded to take her soon, while he is still within reach."

"This is getting to be quite an order our girl is being handed. Now, not only does she have to fool these people, learn all about them and their organization, whatever it is, and make her getaway, she's got to escape with a helpless Ph.D. on her back."

"Dr. Michaelis isn't quite helpless. As a matter of fact, he's well under fifty, athletic, and considered handsome in some quarters."

"Sure. They're all personality kids, these days, and in a tough spot I'd trade them all for one ugly old-timer with store teeth or no teeth at all."

Mac said, as if there had been no interruption, "And I am not ordering Jean to escape with Dr. Michaelis, even if she does have the good fortune to reach him."

I looked at him. "I'm kind of slow, sir. You have to bring me along by easy stages."

"If she can rescue him, that will be fine," Mac said quietly, "but as you point out, it could well turn out to be an impossible task."

"So?"

"Jean's orders are quite simple and specific," Mac said. "You may as well know what they are; they apply to you if by some remote chance you should find yourself in a position to carry them out." He looked at me over the desk. "Our instructions specify only that the knowledge in Dr. Michaelis' head must not leave the country," he said deliberately. "How to achieve this result is left entirely to the discretion of the agent on the spot. No questions will be asked. Do you understand?"

I drew a long breath. "Yes, sir," I said. "I understand."

3

Waiting in the motel room, I did not think about this. It wasn't something you'd pick to while away the lonely minutes, and it was Jean's problem, anyway.

Instead, I glanced at the wrinkled paper to pass the time, and learned that a hurricane named Eloise was giving Florida a tough time; it had been expected when I came through from Cuba. The paper didn't say how far north it might be felt. Well, bad weather is usually an advantage, if anything, in our line of work; besides, I hoped to be through with the job long before the storm had time to work its way up the coast—through, and on my way to Texas.

I tossed the paper aside and thought about Gail Hendricks. To be sure, our date had been very tentative— as tentative as the leave that had been promised me after the last assignment—but I'd made the mistake of wiring that things looked promising when I first hit Washington, and now I'd had to wire again. She wasn't any Penelope to wait years for her Ulysses.

I heard my people coming well before they reached the door. There were two of them, as I'd been told there would be. The man was delivering Jean right on the dot of ten-thirty, as he was supposed to. She was giving him a loud, drunken argument, as she was supposed to. They paused outside long enough to let me rise and take shelter in the bathroom. Then the door opened.

"I'm all right, I tell you!" Jean was protesting. Her voice was slurred. "Won't you please, please, *please* leave me the hell alone? The way you hang around watching me, anybody'd think I was sick or something—or that somebody didn't trust me!"

The man sounded reasonably sober. He had a young, embarrassed voice. "It's not that, Jean. It's just, well, I'm supposed to stick around and, well, help you through this phase."

"Just because some snoop saw me taking a little drinkie, I've got to have a guardian!" she complained. "What's the matter, is somebody afraid I'm going to talk too much, or something? What I do to my liver is my own damn business!"

"Please, Jean. Not so loud. Here, let me—"

"Keep your cotton-picking hands off me!" Her footsteps came across the room unsteadily. I heard the bottle rattle against the glass as she poured herself a drink. "Not so loud!" she mimicked. "You're always telling me not so loud! Don't drink so much, don't talk so loud. Like a nice little boy saying please Mama don't make another scene. How old are you, anyway, honey? I swear you make me feel like Mrs. Methuselah!"

The young male voice was stiffly self-conscious. "I don't really think my age is pertinent to the discussion."

"Pertinent!" She laughed. "Well, I'll talk as loud as I damn please, hear? And I'll talk about what I please! I'll even talk about—Do you know what folks in the know call that house in Washington we operate out of? They call it Murderers' Row, that's what they call it, and a damn good name, too! But we're not supposed to talk about that, are we? Not even in whispers, heavens no! We're not supposed to talk about the house, and if we go there, we can't drive straight to the door even if it's raining. Oh, no, we've got to get out blocks away and make sure nobody's following—"

"Please, Jean! This room hasn't been checked. It may be wired for all we know!"

She paid him no attention. "—and we mustn't ever, ever tell anybody what we really do, not on your life! And of course we mustn't say a word about the horrible gray man who sits in that upstairs office in front of that bright window and sends us out to—no, I won't shut up! If people only knew the dreadful things that are done in the name of peace and democracy! Horrible things!"

I heard her gulp at her drink. The man said hastily, "All right, Jean. All right. We'll talk about it when you're not—when you're feeling better. I'll be going now, but I'll be right next door as soon as I've had a cup of coffee. Call me if you need me. Remember, we're all trying to help you. Just don't make it too hard for us."

"If thatsh a threat," she said thickly, "if that's a threat, to hell with you, honey! You don't scare me a bit. You don't scare me one little bitty bit, hear?"

"I didn't mean—good night, Jean." He seemed to hesitate. "I—er, good night."

He moved away. The door opened and closed behind him. I glanced at my watch. It read ten-forty. His timing was good and he'd delivered his lines pretty well. But Mac had been right. This was, of course, the kid with the weak stomach—code name Alan—who'd refused to do the job; and I was ready to agree that he'd have botched it. It wasn't a job for a sentimental kid; particularly not a sentimental kid who, by his voice, was desperately in love with the somewhat older agent he'd been assigned to watch.

I now had twenty minutes while he drank his coffee, before witnesses. I pushed the bathroom door aside and went in there. She was standing by the big bed, swaying slightly. From the information I'd been given, the appearance of her room, and the sound of her voice, I'd expected a sodden female bum, but she looked surprisingly good, considering.

She was wearing a simple, long-sleeved black dress with a lot of pearls at the throat—the kind of standard dress-up outfit in which they can look reasonably well-groomed as long as they can stay on their feet and keep their stockings up. She was obviously loaded, sure, but at first glance she looked just like an attractive suburban housewife who'd overestimated her capacity at somebody's cocktail party and would be dreadfully embarrassed in the morning, wondering if anybody'd noticed.

Upon further examination, of course, I could see that the attractive picture was terribly out of focus in a very fundamental way. This wasn't just a pretty woman who'd had one too many, slightly rumpled, apologetic, and appealing. This was—or seemed to be—a real lush, going downhill fast.

"Hello, Jean," I said, coming forward.

She waited for me to reach her, and looked up. Most women have to, even the tall ones, and she wasn't very tall. She had soft, light-brown hair, a little mussed now, and bright, baby-blue eyes, a little bloodshot. Her hands made a clumsy, mechanical gesture towards tidying the hair, while the eyes searched my face.

I guess she'd been wondering what kind of a guy would be sent to do the job friend Alan had turned down. She'd agreed to have the operation, but she wanted to know that the surgeon was a capable man. It was a reasonable attitude; but she looked hard enough and long enough for me to wonder if she'd forgotten her lines. Then she moistened her lips with her tongue, and said, as she was supposed to, "Who—who are you?"

"Never mind names," I said. "You can call me Eric if you like. A man in Washington asked me to look you up. He's disappointed in you, Jean, very disappointed indeed."

"What—what do you want?"

There was a nice note of drunken apprehension in her

voice, but she shouldn't have worn those pearls. Close up, I could see that they were too big and perfect to be real, just costume jewelry; nevertheless their luster made her skin look gray and tired. Well, maybe that was the idea.

I felt very sorry for her. The worst assignments aren't the ones requiring you to do something nasty; the worst assignments are the ones demanding that you *be* something nasty, maybe for weeks or months at a time. I'd been through it myself, and I knew the humiliation she must be feeling, seeing herself through a sober stranger's eyes: a sloppy, swaying figure of disintegration and decay. *One day*, she'd be thinking, *one day I'll show this supercilious jerk what I'm really like—that is if I can ever be human again.*

It was hard to remember that this unpleasant playacting had a purpose, that it was necessary because a certain man was thought to be held somewhere for eventual transport overseas, with knowledge in his head that threatened the national security. It was hard to remember that this woman, who looked hardly capable of putting herself to bed, was supposed to reach Dr. Norman Michaelis, somehow, and either rescue or destroy him before he could be made to talk about an invention with the unlikely name of AUDAP.

I didn't have any faith in her chances of effecting a rescue single-handed, and I doubted that she did. That left her pretty well committed to the unpleasant alternative, after which she was supposed to get away—extricate herself, as Mac had put it—to tell us all about it. If she couldn't make it, she knew what to do. In the armed forces, you're supposed to be brave, if captured, and tell nothing under any circumstances but your name, rank, and serial number. We're not required to be that brave, thank God. We're merely required to kill ourselves.

It wasn't a future to which anyone would look forward with joy, and I could understand the resignation in her blue eyes. I spoke the lines I had been given to memorize.

"I think you know what I want, Jean. I'm sorry, I really am. Everybody goes through bad periods. It's a lousy, dirty business, and we understand and sympathize, up to a point."

"A point?" she whispered. "What point?"

I said, "It wasn't nice of you to fool the kid who just left. It wasn't nice, Jean, and it wasn't smart. Why do you think we sent a green youngster to keep an eye on an experienced operative like you? When you seduced him and tricked him—and made contact with certain other people right under his nose—when you did that, you crossed a line. You gave yourself away. We'd been wondering about you. You told us what we needed to know."

She gasped, "But I haven't really *done*—I haven't really told them—I never meant to go through with—" She swallowed hard. "I was just—a little crazy, I guess."

"It is," I said, deliberately, "a form of insanity that we can't afford to tolerate. I'm sorry."

Don't blame us for the dialogue. Somebody wrote it for us in Washington. Jean stared at me for a moment longer. Her eyes were that china-blue color that never looks real in anyone's but a child's face. They disturbed me, and I saw another disturbing thing: the glass, which she'd kept hidden from me, was full to within an inch of the top with straight whisky—it had to be that, since there was no water nearer than the bathroom, and she hadn't gone in there.

She looked at me, with those odd, blue, child's eyes staring out of the pretty, plump, dissipated woman's face. Then she ducked her head abruptly, and drank down the contents of the glass, shuddered, and set the glass aside. It took her a moment to catch her breath after that massive slug. Well, if she wanted to anesthetize herself at this point, having said almost everything she was supposed to say, I couldn't really blame her.

She licked her lips, and got out her final line with difficulty, "I know—I know, you're going to—to kill me!"

"Not kill, Jean," I said. "Not kill."

As I went to work, I was glad for her sake that she had all that alcohol inside her, but I wished she'd stuck to those corduroy pants. She was still kind of attractive in spite of everything. Nicely dressed as she was, it was kind of like taking an axe to the Mona Lisa.

I wasn't halfway through the scientifically brutal roughing-up program Dr. Perry had laid out for me when she died.

4

It wasn't the worst moment of my life. After all, I've been responsible for the deaths of people I knew and liked: it happens in the business. Although we'd worked for the same outfit, this woman had been a stranger to me. Still, she'd trusted me to know what I was doing, and it's no fun to find yourself holding a corpse and wondering what the hell went wrong.

I caught her as she collapsed, and I felt her fight for breath—for life—and fail to make it. It took only a moment. Then she was dead. I was clumsy about easing her to the floor; I got my watch strap tangled in her necklace. Maybe I was just a bit rattled, too. Anyway, suddenly there were artificial pearls all over the rug. Several strands had been broken by the time I'd managed to lay her down and disentangle myself. The damn beads kept slipping off the broken strings by twos and threes, and rolling about in a nasty alive way while she lay among them, absolutely still. Edgar Allen Poe would have thought it was swell.

I straightened up and took a couple of long breaths and listened. She'd died practically in silence, but it had been a very loud silence, if you know what I mean; and there had been a bit of scuffling before that. It seemed as if somebody outside must have noticed something, but apparently nobody had.

I took another long breath, and knelt down and made a brief examination. There was nothing fundamentally wrong, that I could see, except that she was dead. She was kind of a mess by this time, of course. She was supposed to be. That was what I was there for. The idea had been for her to look spectacularly beat-up—to show how seriously we took her disloyalty—without having anything really broken except a certain bone in the forearm. As Mac had said, she had to have at least one broken bone or they wouldn't buy it. Besides, a nice big cast makes a person look very harmless and helpless, while at the same time it affords concealment for a number of small emergency tools and weapons, properly designed. The surgeon at the local hospital had his instructions...

But I hadn't got that far when she keeled over; and a woman doesn't die from a bruised eye or a cut lip. She doesn't die from a split dress seam or a laddered stocking. I'd been following instructions carefully. Except for the incidental damage to her clothes and necklace, nothing was broken, and she'd lost no significant amounts of blood. She was just dead, lying there.

I rose and went over and sniffed the glass she'd set aside. It smelled of whisky and nothing else. I uncapped the bottle she'd used and tasted the contents cautiously. If there was an adulterant, it had the flavor of whisky, or no flavor at all. Of course, she could have been given something slow-acting in a drink before she came in here, or in her food, if she'd eaten. Or she could have been shot with a poisoned dart, or stuck with a hypo, or bitten by a black widow spider. Or she could simply have died of heart failure.

I grimaced. Matt Helm, boy detective. It didn't matter what she'd died of, for the moment: she was dead. Scratch Jean, agent, female, five feet four, a hundred and thirty pounds. I went to the door and paused to check my watch band for telltale fibers, and my pockets and pants cuffs for beads. I kicked a slim black shoe out of the way, reflecting absently that I'd never yet met a woman, pro or amateur, who could stay in her pumps when the going got rough.

I looked back. If you can do it, you can damn well look at it, no matter how badly you've loused it up. I never trust these delicate chaps who are hell behind a telescopic sight at five hundred yards but can't bear to come up close and see the blood. I gave her a long look, lying there among her spilled pearls. What did I think about—besides wondering, again, what the hell went wrong? Well, if you must know, I thought it would be nice to be in Texas, which is a hell of an attitude, for a good New Mexican.

I went out, pulled the door closed behind me, removed my gloves and put them in my pocket. I turned and walked casually towards my parked car. As I did so, I realized there were people at the pool.

We'd counted on the pool being empty after dark, this time of year. I'd gone too far to turn back without attracting attention; so I sauntered by in a leisurely way, and even allowed myself to glance in that direction, like any man curious about what kind of fools would want to go swimming this late on a cool fall night. An athletic male was doing a racing crawl down the pool. On shore there was another man and two girls. These three were making a funny, funny thing of how cold the air was, how cold the water was, and how cold they were.

Maybe I shouldn't have looked at all, though it seemed like the natural thing to do. Maybe I just looked too long. Anyway, the smaller of the two girls glanced around and, seeing me, gestured for me to stop. I couldn't very well pretend I hadn't noticed. I stopped, like any man flagged down by a pretty girl. I waited. She came up to the low fence that separated the tiled pool area from the concrete walk.

"M-mister, have you g-got a m-m-match?"

The cigarette between her blue-cold lips bobbed as she spoke. She had good reason to be cold; she didn't have enough on to warm a newborn kitten. Personally, I applaud the return of the reasonably discreet one-piece bathing suit, such as the other girl was wearing. It has brought a little suspense back into our lives. For a while, there was hardly a thing a girl could reveal to you in private that you hadn't already seen in public—you and every other man on the beach.

But this kid was still on the Bikini kick. The scanty bra and G-string might have looked very sexy in July, but they didn't go well with goose-bumps. They just looked ridiculous and a bit indecent. I got a folder of matches from my pocket and held it out. She waved her hands to indicate that they were wet. She leaned forward, sticking her face, and the cigarette, over the railing.

I struck a match and stepped up to hold it for her, having no choice. This close, I realized how small she was: no more than five feet and maybe ninety pounds of toy blonde. Her hair, cut boyishly short, was that pale color that doesn't even darken much when wet. It was plastered unbecomingly to her small head. Even so, soaked, shivering and practically naked, she was cute. You wanted to drop a handkerchief over her when nobody was looking, and slip her into your pocket, and take her home for a pet.

"Thanks!" she said, throwing back her head and blowing smoke at the night sky. "I gu-guess you think we're d-drunk or c-crazy. Funny thing is, you're p-perfectly right!"

I grinned at her, in response, and walked away. I got into the car and took out a handkerchief and wiped my hands, which were slightly damp with perspiration—I'd half-expected somebody to start yelling murder while I stood there being polite and helpful. I started the little blue Ford they'd given me. Lash Petroni would drive something flashy on his own time, but he'd want an inconspicuous heap when he was working. I backed out of the slot and started towards the highway. I had to remind myself not to attract attention by hurrying.

The little blonde, wrapping herself in a striped beach towel under the pool lights, paused to wave at me as I drove past. She wasn't only cute, she was friendly, too. Under the circumstances, I may be forgiven for preferring the attitude of the other girl, the lean, dark, reserved one, who wouldn't demean herself by bumming matches from strangers. Well, time would tell how much damage had been done, if any.

It didn't take much time. I didn't even get halfway to Washington before I was picked up.

5

When I heard the siren and saw the red flasher coming up in the mirror, I glanced at the speedometer to make sure I was operating within the law and held on, hoping they'd go past to bother somebody else. They didn't. I pulled over onto the shoulder, therefore, like a docile citizen, and cranked down the window, waiting for the first policeman to come up.

"What's the matter, officer?" I asked.

Then I saw the revolver in his hand, and I knew I was in real trouble. They don't unlimber the firearms for a simple traffic offense. I'd been hoping to make Washington, where I'd have turned in the car for burial, along with everything else connected with the fictitious Lash Petroni, who'd have ceased to exist. That was the first line of defense, if things went wrong. The second was to stick to my Petroni cover and hope for the best.

The one thing I had no authority to do was to reveal myself publicly as a government agent who went around beating up people—not to mention leaving them dead on the floor. That decision was Mac's to make, not mine.

I had no choice. I drew a long breath and became Lash Petroni until further notice. "I asked you a question, buddy," I said harshly as the state policeman reached me. "What's the big idea, stopping me like this? I wasn't doing over fifty-five, and what's with the crummy artillery, anyway? Here's my license—"

"Please keep your hands on the steering wheel, sir." He was very polite and business-like. He waited until his partner was in position to back him up before he waved me out with the gun. "Now get out slowly—"

They drove me back the way I'd come. Presently they left the big highway and took me by smaller roads to a building equipped with a tall radio mast, where they turned me over to the county police, with a sigh of relief. They were state cops. Their primary job was seeing that people didn't kill themselves, or each other, on the public highways. Suspected criminals, even loud-mouthed ones, were just a sideline with them.

The county officers searched me and put me through the fingerprint routine. They also searched the little Ford, which had been brought around by somebody. At least I deducted that was what a couple of them had been doing outside when they came back in with my suitcase— Lash Petroni's suitcase, to be exact. Mine reposed in a Washington hotel room that was beginning to seem more remote every minute. As for Texas, it was already as unattainable as paradise.

They went through the bag and discovered the switchblade knife hidden in the lining. That had been Mac's idea. When helping an agent build a cover for a particular assignment, he's apt to get carried away by creative enthusiasm. I'd thought the knife unnecessary as a prop, but it's always reassuring to have some weapon along, so I hadn't fought it very hard. Maybe I should have. It certainly didn't make the police feel more kindly towards me now, although it did convince them of my low character.

Then we waited. I offered my blustering Petroni act again, got no takers, and subsided on a bench in sullen silence. After a while, the door opened, and a man came in. He was stocky and white-haired, with a heavy, impassive cop face. His uniform was neat enough, but it had seen lots of wear.

"Here you are, Tom," one of the office help said. "Name: James A. Peters, Chicago. About six-four, about two hundred, dark suit and hat—well, look for yourself. Picked up at eleven-seventeen about twenty miles west on U.S. 50, driving a blue Falcon two-door, Illinois plates."

"That checks right down the line." Neither policeman looked at me, but I didn't think it was accidental that I was present to overhear the conversation. I was being informed, I gathered, that they had the goods on me and I might as well confess. "What's this?" the white-haired man asked, touching the knife on the counter.

"We found it in his luggage, hidden behind the lining."

The white-haired one picked up the knife and carried

it over to me. He stood over me for a moment without speaking, tossing the knife contemptuously into the air and catching it again—closed, of course, or he'd have cut himself badly. He was probably pretty good with his police revolver, and maybe even with his bare hands, but knives were out of his line and he was proud of it.

So many of them are, these days. Jim Bowie would be startled to hear it, as would Jim Bridger and Kit Carson and all the rest of those rugged old-timers who opened up a wilderness with their Arkansas toothpicks and Green River blades; but nowadays there's supposed to be something very underhanded and un-American about a knife.

"I'm Sergeant Crowell," the white-haired man said. "Tom Crowell."

"If you drop that," I said, "and damage it, you'll buy me a new one."

He caught the knife and looked at it again, raising his eyebrows. "You admit it's yours?"

"Damn right it's mine," I said. "And I want it back, along with my cuff links and cigarette case and all the rest of the stuff those jerks have been pawing through like they owned it."

"A knife like this is illegal," he said.

"Be your age, Sergeant," I said. "Wearing it may be illegal in certain places, but you know as well as I do that in my suitcase, locked in the car trunk—hell, I could carry a Samurai sword back there if I wanted. Legally."

He sighed. "I guess that's true, Mr. Peters. But it's kind

of a specialized weapon. Do you mind telling me why you have it?"

"I'm interested in specialized weapons; it's a hobby of mine." I got to my feet, which gave me a sudden height advantage of several inches. He was heavier, though. But he wouldn't be hard to take. Nobody is who kids himself that one deadly weapon is morally better, or worse, than another. I said, "Did you have the state boys flag me down and bring me here just because you heard I was packing a shiv in my suitcase? What's the matter, did some local taxpayer get cut? Send it to your lab, if you've got one. They won't find any blood on it."

He looked at me sharply. We both knew that knife was irrelevant—that it had nothing whatever to do with the case—but I wasn't supposed to know it, yet. He tried to decide whether or not my attitude indicated guilty information. Then he shook his head, dismissing the subject.

"Would you mind telling me where you've spent the day, Mr. Peters?"

I said, "I was a day early for an appointment in Washington, so I took a drive over your big bridge and down the peninsula a ways, just sight-seeing. I was coming back to Washington to spend the night when I was stopped." Saying it, I wondered if there were some way he could check if I'd crossed the toll bridge twice. Usually there isn't; but I took a step forward and said harshly, to get us off the subject, "What the hell is this all about, anyway? Who do you think you're pushing

around? You hick cops are all alike when you get hold of
somebody with an out-of-state license—"

I could have saved my indignation. He had stopped
listening. Another policeman had stuck his head in
the door. When Crowell looked in his direction, the
newcomer nodded briefly and withdrew as silently as
he had appeared. Crowell tossed the knife into my open
suitcase and turned to me.

"Let's go in the other office, Mr. Peters."

"I'm not going anywhere until somebody tells me
what—"

He took my arm. "If you please. This way."

I jerked free and started to speak. Then the door
opened and stayed that way, held by the young policeman
who had looked in a moment ago. Two people came in.
The woman stopped abruptly, staring at me.

"That's him!" she said. "That's the murderer!"

6

It wasn't exactly a shattering surprise. The police had been too sure of themselves not to have what they considered positive identification.

The surprise was that it wasn't the diminutive Bikini blonde whose cigarette I'd lit. This was the taller female member of the Polar Bear Club; the one who'd seemed to pay me no attention at the pool. She'd exchanged her bathing suit for a casually expensive-looking sweater-and-skirt outfit, and she looked older and more dignified with clothes on, but she still looked quite tall: a brown, handsome woman with dark hair brought back smoothly to a big knot at the nape of her neck.

I already had reason not to be fond of the lady—even with justification, nobody likes to be called a murderer—but seeing her at close range for the first time, I couldn't help that special feeling of respect and admiration reserved for something unique. I mean, one gets tired of the sexy young carbon copies of Marilyn Monroe and

Brigitte Bardot; one even gets bored with all the nice girls who used to be more or less Grace Kelly and are now more or less Jacqueline Kennedy, attractive though the prototypes may be.

This woman wasn't outstandingly beautiful or strikingly seductive, but there was only one of her. She'd never look like anybody else. She had a real nose in her face, instead of something cute and indeterminate. She had a real mouth with real teeth—strong, white ones—and real eyes with real eyebrows. She was herself. It takes a certain amount of guts, these days. But it was no time to stand gawking at handsome ladies.

"Murderer?" I said sharply. "Who's a murderer? You can't pin anything like that on me!" I whirled on Crowell. "Listen, what kind of an identification do you call this? I've got a right to a proper line-up—"

"I'm trying very hard to protect your rights, Mr. Peters," the white-haired man told me. "I asked you to go into the other office, remember? You refused." He turned to the newcomers. "You're sure, Mrs. Rosten?"

"Quite sure."

"And you, Mr. Rosten?"

The man hesitated. He'd been at the pool, too; a dark, well-built chap with gray at the temples, very distinguished in appearance. Like the woman, he had the smooth rich tan you get by working at that and not much else. He also had the air of a man who'd achieved nothing in life except marrying money.

"I—I don't really know," he said.

"Of course you do, Louis," he was told by his wife. "Why, there's no possible doubt. That's the man!"

"I was looking the other way," he said uncertainly. "Also, I was freezing. I was just vaguely aware that Teddy had gone over to get a light from somebody walking by—"

"Vaguely!" she snapped. "Well, that's typical!"

He flushed, drew himself up, and turned stiffly to Crowell. "I'm afraid I can't help you, officer. As I told you before, I never got a good look at him. I don't think Billy did, either. He was still in the pool, showing off the stroke that brought victory to dear old Whatsis only a few years back."

"Billy?" Crowell consulted a notebook. "That would be Mr. William Orcutt, the other lady's escort?"

"Yes, I told you. He's a local boy—the Annapolis Orcutts, you know. As a matter of fact, he's my wife's nephew. We drafted him to entertain our little visitor for the evening. We had dinner at home, and then some vigorous person suggested a swim—"

"You did, Louis," Mrs. Rosten said.

"I did not, my dear. I thought it was a ridiculous idea, considering the weather, but I was out-voted—Anyway, Sergeant, our pool has been drained, so we came to the motel, changed in Teddy's room, and exposed ourselves to the elements briefly. Then the kids jumped into their clothes and went on to some fascinating place Billy knew about—unfortunately, I've forgotten the name. We dressed more slowly and called home for a car, but if it ever arrived, it got lost in the confusion. Maybe you know something about it?"

"I'll check. Don't worry about it, sir. We'll see that you get home all right."

Mrs. Rosten said, "I suppose you'll want a statement or something. I'll be glad to sign it; but would you mind terribly if we got started on it?"

"Right away, ma'am. I—" He stopped, as the young policeman who'd brought in the Rostens came back into the office. "What is it, Egan?"

Egan stepped up and whispered something in Crowell's ear. Crowell nodded.

"Excuse me, ma'am," he said to Mrs. Rosten, and he turned to me. "This way—"

I trotted out my Petroni act. He paid no attention to it, but marched me back down a hall to a smaller room that looked like a waiting room with wooden chairs set along the walls. The room was empty, which surprised me. I'd expected another confrontation. Crowell gestured towards a chair and we sat down facing a door that had opaque glass in the upper half. At least it was opaque from our side. This made more sense.

I said, "Who the hell do you think you're fooling, Crowell? One-way glass, yet? Wait till my lawyer gets up in court and tells how you cops tried to railroad me!"

"Policemen," he said.

"What?"

"We don't like that other word," he said. "We prefer to be called policemen, particularly by goons like you, Petroni."

I'd been Mr. Peters up to now. I said sullenly, "So you've got word from Chi. So what?"

"You're Jimmy Petroni, known as Jimmy the Lash. You're pretty small time, but you sometimes run errands for the big boys."

"Who's small time?" I asked angrily. "Let me tell you—"

"Later," he said. "Later, you're going to tell me lots of things, Petroni. Right now you're going to shut up. When I tell you, you're going to get up and walk around. All right. Up. Walk."

I rose sullenly. There was a sound in the hall outside, the rapping sound of high heels. A man's voice spoke out there.

"Don't be afraid, miss. He can't see you."

"Who's afraid?" It was the voice of the girl who'd asked me for a match; it seemed like a long time ago. I drew a long breath. It had been too much to hope that they'd get drunk and hit a culvert at ninety miles an hour before the police could find them and bring them here. Anyway, one dead woman was enough for one night. The clear, high voice spoke again. "Well, he does look sort of familiar, but I can't really see—"

The doorknob rattled. The man's voice said quickly, "No, miss, you're not supposed to go in!"

Then she was in. She looked just as small as I remembered her, in a light, summery, full-skirted dress, predominantly blue, and tiny, white, high-heeled shoes. Her short, blonde hair, dry now, was a silvery cap on her small head. She looked child-sized in front of the big policeman who followed her in—without looking the least bit like a child, if you know what I mean.

She came forward. The policeman reached for her clumsily, but Crowell waved him back. The little girl looked up at me. Her eyes were as blue as Jean's had been, I noticed. It didn't seem like a happy omen. She stared at me for quite a long time. I didn't know why she bothered to go through the motions. There was no doubt in my mind that she'd recognized me as easily as I'd recognized her.

Crowell spoke. "Well, Miss Michaelis? Is this the man who lit your cigarette at the swimming pool?"

She gave me a final look and turned away. "Oh, no," she said. "No, I've never seen this man before in my life."

That was far from being the end of it, of course. They had Mrs. Rosten in and she said yes. The little girl said no. Mr. Rosten said maybe, maybe not. A plump collegiate type with a crew cut was dragged in and addressed variously as Billy and Mr. Orcutt, depending upon who was speaking. He was no help. He hadn't seen anything but water, he said—damn cold, green, chlorinated water.

I didn't get to listen to all of this at close range. They moved me into another room so they could discuss me more freely, but I guess the forces of law and order were shaken by the unexpected turn of events. A door got left open, and I heard most of it, and filed it for reference. It was too early to try to figure out why a perfectly strange young lady—with a very interesting last name—should get up and lie for me, plausibly and stubbornly. At the moment, I was more interested in learning whether or not her efforts in my behalf would be successful. They were.

When I came outside at last, having been told, that I could leave but that I'd better keep myself available, there was a cold wind blowing from the direction of the Bay. At least it seemed cold to me, after the time I'd spent in Cuba. My car was parked in front of the building, along with an empty police car and a white Thunderbird convertible with the top up. There were people in the Thunderbird. The engine was turning over quietly.

Under other circumstances, seeing a car waiting like that, ready to go, I might have looked for a murderous blast from an automatic weapon and a tire-ripping getaway, but this seemed hardly the time and place for such goings-on. Anyway, the only man with a current reason to wish me dead, as far as I was aware, was waiting in Washington to cut me into small, squirming strips with his tongue. Mac doesn't like having his operations fouled up and his people killed.

I got the keys out of the Falcon's ignition and opened the trunk and threw my suitcase in. Coming back around the car, I almost stepped on the little blonde, who'd come over from the Thunderbird.

"So your name is Petroni," she said, looking up at me. "Jim Petroni."

"There's no law against it," I said.

She laughed softly. "Those policemen certainly wished there was, didn't they?" She continued to speak in the same light tone of voice. "Teddy Michaelis," she said. "The Tidewater Motel. Room seventeen. You know where it is."

"I know the motel," I said. "I can find the room."

"Don't be long," she said.

The college type behind the wheel tapped the horn impatiently. She stared at me for a moment longer, as if fixing my face in her memory to brighten the long, dark, lonely winter nights to come. At least that was the most flattering explanation of her scrutiny; I don't claim it was the right one. Then she ran lightly to the convertible and slid across the seat, reaching back to slam the big door shut. The window was down. I heard her voice clearly.

"Sorry to keep you all waiting; I wanted to be absolutely sure. But you're wrong, Mrs. Rosten; he isn't the one, I'd swear it. And I saw him lots closer than you did."

I heard Mrs. Rosten say from the rear seat, "I still think—"

That was no surprise. She'd keep right on thinking it, too. But her word didn't carry the weight of that of the girl who'd actually spoken to the murderer, which was just as well for me.

I watched them drive away. Then I got into the Falcon and drove in the other direction. It would have been poor technique to appear to be following; and I needed some information and advice before I accepted the little lady's invitation, anyway. Things were looking up. At least I had something with which to draw Mac's attention from my many and serious shortcomings.

It took me a while to get my bearings on the country roads on which I found myself, and a little longer to decide I was being followed. I didn't think it was the police. They'd have managed it less obviously. This was a one-man tailing job, and the guy was damn well not going to lose me whether I spotted him or not.

I sighed, and led him out on a sandy back road, and stopped to see if he wanted to talk. He didn't want to talk. He drove past without slacking speed, as if I was nothing to him but an obstruction by the roadside. I got out and opened up the hood of the Ford. The compact six-cylinder engine looked as if it would have been easy to fix, had there been anything wrong with it. I went back to the trunk and opened that, and fussed around in there for a while. I might have been looking for tools. The guy out in the dark could make up his own story.

He was out there, all right. He wasn't just interested in learning where I was going. He'd parked up ahead and circled back on foot, stalking me. I took a chance on a gun and let him come in. He made the last ten yards in a rush. I pressed the button of the instrument with which I had provided myself, ducked as I turned, and put out my arm.

It worked very nicely. He ran right onto the long, thin blade of the switch-blade knife, held low. The club he was swinging passed over my head. I pulled out the knife and stepped back and clear of the car, ready to thrust again. A blade hasn't got the shocking power of a bullet. I might still have a fight on my hands.

I needn't have worried. He was through for the night. He dropped the club and put both hands to his stomach and looked down fearfully, as if expecting a horrible display of gushing blood and torn entrails. There was, of course, nothing of the sort. I'd done a clean, tidy job. After making sure of this, he looked up reproachfully. The light from the sky caught his face. I'd never met him before, although we'd come close earlier in the evening; but I'd seen his picture and read his official description in Washington. It just wasn't my night for being right. On top of my other goofs, I'd miscalculated badly when I figured there was only one man around who'd like me to drop dead because of the way I'd loused up the night's work. I'd forgotten Alan, our tender-hearted, lovesick young man in Maryland.

7

He was a good-looking kid, if you like them with dark, wavy hair and soulful expressions. Well, agents are needed in all shapes and sizes, and I suppose Mac had use for a pretty boy when he took this one on.

I got a gun off him: the standard little sawed-off, aluminum-framed, five-shot Smith and Wesson .38 that's issued to us whenever the job doesn't require anything esoteric in the way of firearms. You can get the equivalent Colt if you insist. It shoots six times but is a little harder to hide, being that much thicker. The general feeling is, if you can't do it with five shots, you probably can't do it at all.

Then I picked up the club he'd tried to use on me. It was a kindo stick, a kind of overgrown policeman's billy, with a leather wrist loop, only you don't use it around the wrist. You just loop it over your thumb a certain way, easy to release, so that the man who grabs the stick hasn't got you, too. Of course, taking a stick away from a good Japanese-trained kindo man doesn't come under the heading of healthful exercise. The karate and judo experts, who'll cheerfully go up against a knife, will back off from a thirty-inch stick in the hands of a man who knows how to use it.

I tossed it into the car. It was kind of pitiful, actually. They come out of training having learned a few miraculous chops with the edge of the hand, a few blows with a magic stick, and they think they're invulnerable and invincible.

I said, "Very poor technique, Alan. You sounded like a bull elk coming through the brush, and your attack was lousy. Why didn't you use the gun?"

He didn't answer. He just stood there holding his stomach with both hands, staring at me sullenly.

I asked, "How were you planning to explain all the weapons to the cops?"

He licked his lips. "I have a license for the gun. I was supposed to have brought it along to protect Jean—she was going under the name of Ellington, Mrs. Laura Ellington. She was supposed to have been threatened by somebody, somebody in her past. She wouldn't tell me the details; she pleaded with me not to ask questions, just help her hide out in a safe place until—" He shrugged imperceptibly. "That was the cover story I was supposed to give out after I discovered that she'd been—attacked."

"But you didn't give out?"

He spoke dully. "When I came in, she was dead. I—I guess I lost my head. There were some people from one of the units who'd seen you leave. I told them to call the police. I started after you. When I caught up with you, you'd already been arrested by the state troopers. I just—followed, hoping for a chance—" He stopped.

"Sure," I said. "Well, get in the car."

He was still holding himself. He didn't want to move. He was afraid he'd fall apart if he moved. I shrugged, closed the trunk and the hood, got in and started the motor.

"Make up your mind," I said. "Stay here if you like. I'm leaving now."

He came around the car, walking very gingerly. I opened the door for him. He eased himself to the seat. I didn't really like reaching across him to close the door—he could have been shamming—but he didn't take advantage of the opening. I started the car.

"Where—" He licked his lips and started over. "Where are you taking me?"

"To the nearest phone. For advice and assistance. Watch the roads so you can tell them how to pick up your car." I glanced at him. "It might help if you told me precisely what's bugging you, to use the vernacular."

"Why," he said, surprised, "why, you killed her!" He turned to look at me. "Didn't you?"

"Well," I said, "she died."

"She wasn't supposed to die! You killed her!"

I started to speak again, and stopped. There was no point in arguing about it. What he thought didn't really matter any more, anyway. He was hospital-bound and out of it. There were other people whose opinions were of

more importance to me, one person in particular. I hoped
he'd be more open-minded on the subject, but I wasn't
really counting on it.

I found an all-night filling station with a phone booth.
I parked the Falcon by the booth, since there was no
reason to be coy.

"Don't move," I said to Alan, "don't talk, and don't
think—there's no really good evidence that you know
how. If you have to die, do it quietly."

He gave me a look full of hate, sitting there holding
himself. That was all right. He was mad enough to stay
alive if he could manage, which was the way I wanted to
keep him. I glanced at my watch as I got out of the car,
and saw that he'd already made it for seventeen minutes.
Wounded there, they go pretty fast if they go at all.
Apparently none of the major abdominal blood vessels
had been damaged, which gave him a good chance of
surviving, properly cared for.

I closed the door of the booth behind me. The light
came on, making me feel like an illuminated target at the
end of a long, dark rifle range. I couldn't help wondering
how many other dangerous characters I'd casually
overlooked, with hatred in their hearts for one M. Helm.
Well, they'd just have to line up and await their turns.

I put my coin into the slot, got the operator, and told
her the number. A minute or so later I had Mac on the
wire. There's a rumor to the effect that he does sleep, but
nobody's ever caught him at it, to my knowledge.

"Eric here," I said. "Is Dr. Perry just our beating-up

specialist, or does he know about belly wounds, too?"

He didn't ask any foolish questions. He just gave me the answer. "Dr. Perry is a capable all-around surgeon."

I said, "Well, you'd better load him into a fast car with a good driver. Send them east out of Washington on U.S. 50. Tell Perry it's a puncture wound a few inches below the navel. The weapon was approximately half an inch wide by six inches long, clean and sharp. It went in most of the way. I have some other things to report, but as soon as I hang up here, I'll head for the big highway and come west towards Washington at the legal speed—considering the state of my passenger, I don't want to attract attention by driving faster. Give them a description of my car and tell them to flash their lights twice when they see me in the other lane. Okay. I'll wait while you get them going, sir."

"Very well."

I stood at the silent phone, looking out through the glass of the booth. The filling station wasn't doing much business at this hour. In the little Ford, Alan sat motionless, staring straight ahead. Presently Mac came back on the line.

"It's a 3.8 Jaguar sedan," he said. "The parking lights burn when the headlights are on, European fashion: two small lights below and slightly outside two large ones. They will be coming fast, so they want you to keep your car's interior light on for easier identification."

"That'll cut my vision down," I said. "They'll have to do the spotting."

"They are prepared to," he said. "The description of the weapon corresponds with a knife recently issued to you. I gather you didn't fall on it yourself."

I said, "Hell, I haven't cut myself on one of my own knives since I was a kid. It's Alan, sir. He came for me with a club. I gather he calls it love."

There was a little pause. "Couldn't you have handled him with less damage, Eric?"

I could see my face in the glass of the booth. It looked lean and hard and ugly—that is to say, it looked pretty much as usual. "I told you, he was trying to scramble my brains."

"Even so, it seems a little drastic." Mac hesitated briefly. "You seem to have had a busy evening, Eric. I've had a call from Chicago. They, in turn, have had a call from the county authorities near Annapolis, Maryland. About a certain Mr. Peters, alias Petroni. The word murder was mentioned. Perhaps you'd care to explain."

I said, "The patient died on the operating table, sir."

"So I gathered, after making cautious inquiries. You were arrested, I understand?"

"Yes, sir, but they turned me loose."

"Well, that's something." His voice was dry. "What's Alan's condition?"

"Pretty good, I'd say. No signs of excessive internal hemorrhage. With surgery and antibiotics, he ought to make it."

"Yes. Nevertheless, he will be incapacitated for weeks, maybe months. And Jean is dead. What happened there? Did your hand slip?"

"I don't think so, sir. She just gave a little gasp and folded up. By the time I'd caught her and eased her to the floor, she was dead."

"There was no heart condition. Dr. Perry checked her thoroughly. Jean was physically sound."

"And psychologically?"

"What do you mean?"

"She was scared," I said. "She didn't like what she had to face, either at my hands or the opposition's. She'd had it, sir. She was sick of looking in the mirror and seeing a drunken slob. She could hardly face the thought of looking in the mirror and seeing a beatup drunken slob. As for the rest of the job—well, I have a hunch she was simply trying not to think of it at all."

"Dr. Klein examined her, too, and passed her."

"Who's Klein, our new psychiatrist? They come and they go, don't they? Well, I have no degree in any branch of medicine, but I know a scared and fed-up female when I see one, sir."

Mac said coldly, "Jean was a good agent and an excellent actress. She was supposed to act frightened and shaky. What are you trying to say, Eric? That it wasn't your fault that she died? That she simply died of fright?"

I gripped the telephone hard. It was no time to get mad. It never is. "No, sir," I said. "It was my job and my responsibility, sure. I simply don't believe I killed her by hitting her too hard. I don't think my hand slipped. I'd like an investigation."

"It will certainly be investigated, as soon as we can

confer with the local authorities without the risk of publicity. I'm told an autopsy will be performed. I'll try to get a copy of the findings. But in the meantime we have Jean dead and Alan seriously injured, at your hands. That is two agents put out of commission in one night, Eric. The enemy seldom does better."

"No, sir," I said. "Maybe I should have gone to Texas."

The minute I said it, meaning only to say something suitably humble and rueful, I knew it was a mistake. I knew it by the quality of the silence that followed.

"I see," Mac said slowly, at last. "I see. That is how you feel, Eric? That was Dr. Klein's theory. When an agent makes a serious error, as you know, we review his record immediately. I called up Klein at once, when Chicago called me."

I said, "I grant the error. I've got to; Jean's dead. But there's nothing wrong with my record, sir."

"No, except the sheer quantity of it. Since you came back to us, after your wife left you a few years ago, you've had no real time off at all. Fatigue, was Klein's immediate diagnosis."

"The hell with Klein," I said. "We fought the whole damn war without a headshrinker in attendance. And the hell with fatigue, too. I haven't asked for any leave, have I? Not until this time—"

"Precisely," Mac said. "Fatigue and subconscious resentment, Klein said. And, probably, what he referred to as a mild superman complex. I don't like the term, Eric, but I have seen it happen before in men whose occupation allows them to kill and get away with it. After a while, their judgment becomes impaired, since human life has ceased to have much value for them."

I laughed shortly. "Sir, if you're suggesting that I went out and murdered a woman, a fellow agent, simply because I was mad at you for interfering with my love-life—"

"I said the resentment was subconscious, Eric."

"Sure," I said. "Thanks. I love being a subconscious murderer, sir. Let's just skip the analysis, if you don't mind. Right now, I'd better get Alan on the road; but first I'd like to know if Dr. Norman Michaelis, our missing genius, has a sister or daughter—Miss Michaelis was the form of address used. Age twenty plus, height five feet minus, say ninety pounds after a heavy meal, silver-blonde hair, blue eyes."

Mac hesitated. "There is a daughter. Theodora. But, Eric—"

"Theodora," I said. "That's a lot of name for a little bit of girl. What's the family picture? Is there a wife and mother?"

"The wife and mother died in childbirth. Eric—"

"The daughter is here, sir," I said. "In fact, she got me out of jail by lying her pretty little head off. I have a date to find out why, as soon as I get Alan off my hands. I'll report by phone as soon as—"

"You will," Mac said, "report to me in person, at once."

I frowned at the phone. "But, sir—"

His voice was curt. "Any leads you have will be followed up, you may be sure."

I said slowly, "The invitation was issued to me, as Jim Petroni, alias Jimmy the Lash. The lady has just told the police a great big fib, remember? She's not likely to open her door and her mouth to any old government gumshoe, sir."

"We'll have to risk that. I want you to come in immediately, Eric."

"What's the matter, sir?" I asked. "Are you afraid I'll go completely berserk and give the outfit a bad reputation?"

Saying it, I expected any answer except the little embarrassed silence that followed, that said more plainly than words that that was exactly what he was afraid of. I'd murdered Jean with my subconscious resentment; I'd stuck a hole in Alan. I'd flipped. I was a menace on the loose.

"Let us say," he said carefully, "that Dr. Klein's advice is that you be recalled for examination and possible treatment—probably only rest. It is quite possible that you'll be on your way to Texas tomorrow or the next day. How would you like that?"

"Thanks," I said, "for the lollipop, sir."

"I want you to turn Alan over to Dr. Perry and follow them in. That's an order."

"Yes, sir," I said.

8

I spotted their Jag well ahead of time and flashed an answer to their signal, but they were coming right along, and it took them a while to fire the retro-rockets and get the flaps down and find a place to cross the median to the west-bound lane. In the meantime, I'd pulled the little sedan out to the shoulder to wait for them.

"We were going to be married after she finished this job," Alan said suddenly. It was his first conversational effort in a long time. "Jean's professional pride wouldn't let her quit in the middle of it, but afterwards we were going to get out of this dirty business and be normal human beings for a change. We'd never had a real home, either of us. We were going to make one together."

"Sure," I said. "She'd have been the mother you'd always wanted, and you'd have been the baby she'd yearned for all her life."

His head came around sharply. "You callous beast! Just because she was a little older—"

"Cut it out, Alan," I said.

"I loved her," he said.

"Cut it out," I said. "Go away. Die. Or just shut up."
He started to speak again, but I cut in, "The one thing
you could have done for her, you didn't do. You let a
stranger do it. Then you got mad because it turned out
wrong and went for him with a club. And now, by God,
you start talking about love!" I grimaced. "Do me a
favor. Hemorrhage."

He was staring at me. "You think—you think I should
have done that? To her?"

"Somebody was going to have to do the stinking job
if she was to carry out her assignment. Why not you?
What makes you so damn special?" I looked at him. "If
I loved a woman enough to talk about it, if something
like that simply had to be done, if she really wanted it
done, I'd damn well do it myself and see it was done
right by somebody she knew and trusted. At least I
wouldn't sit across the way wringing my hands while it
was happening, and then take it out on the guy who got
stuck with the lousy operation I was too damn delicate to
perform. Now stay here and brood, while I discuss your
survival problems with the medical profession."

The Jaguar had pulled up behind us. I liked the sound
of it, even idling. They don't put the full-race mill into
the sedan, but it's no truck engine, either. Dr. Perry got
out of the bucket seat beside the driver and came to
meet me as I went back there. The driver, a big man, got
out and went around to get something out of the trunk,

presently disappearing into the darkness. I thought this a little peculiar, but maybe I was not supposed to notice. The car had a buggy-whip antenna for radio-telephone communication. I thought it was probably Mac's personal vehicle.

"How's the patient?" Dr. Perry asked.

"Alive," I said. "Bitter."

"With some justification, I would say."

"I know," I said. "I've already been told I should have treated him more gently. Wait till it's your head he's swinging a stick at from behind."

"I wasn't referring to that," Perry said. "The female agent who died at your hands—I understand there was some emotional involvement."

I looked at him for a moment. The headlights bounced enough light our way that I could see him clearly: a clean-cut young professional man with horn-rimmed glasses, neatly dressed, in good physical condition. I wondered what quirk of psychology or fortune had brought him to us—the Foreign Legion of the undercover services—but it isn't something one asks. Maybe he was just getting himself a wide range of medical experience before settling down to a profitable society practice.

I asked, "Why did Jean die, Dr. Perry?"

He blinked. Obviously, he thought it was a strange question for me to ask. After all, I was the guy who'd killed her, wasn't I?

"Why, I don't know," he said. "I wasn't there, how could I say? I rather assumed—" He stopped, embarrassed.

"That my hand slipped? It seems to be a common assumption in these parts," I said. "And a convenient one, for some people."

"If you're implying there was something wrong with Jean—"

I said, "Obviously, there was something wrong. With Jean, or you, or me, or somebody else. She's dead. Maybe you should have examined my hands before clearing me for the job, Doctor. You might have prevented the slip, if there was a slip."

His voice was stiff. "Maybe I should have."

"Maybe," I said, "you should examine them now."

He didn't get it at once. He said impatiently, "Really, I'd better see to my patient—"

"Look at them," I said gently. "The right one is of special interest, Doctor." There was a little silence, as he saw what I was driving at. I said, "Note the weapon. It uses the .38 Special cartridge firing a one-hundred-and-fifty-grain bullet with a muzzle velocity of eleven hundred and fifty feet per second and a muzzle energy of three hundred and sixty-five foot pounds. Now note what happens when I exert pressure on the trigger—"

"Eric." His voice was professionally calm and soothing. "Eric, put the gun away. There's no need for hostility. I am certainly not trying to duck my share of the responsibility for your unfortunate mishap. *Careful!*"

"Don't panic, Doc," I said. "It's a double-action revolver. Not much happens immediately as the trigger moves back, except that the cylinder rotates, bringing a new cartridge into line and the hammer rises, so. This being a pocket pistol, the hammer has no conventional spur, just a little grooved cocking piece that won't hang up in the clothing. Now I catch it with my thumb before the hammer can drop, so."

He couldn't help a sharp intake of breath as the hammer fell a fraction of an inch before being arrested by my thumb.

"Eric—"

I said, "Let us review the situation, Doctor. There is now a loaded cartridge lined up with the firing pin and, of course, with the gun barrel. The trigger is back as far as it will go, rendering all safety devices inoperative. The hammer is fully cocked, held only by my thumb. The muzzle is aimed at your abdomen. The range is about three feet. I ask for your prognosis, Doctor. What will happen when your driver, sneaking up behind me, clouts me alongside the head with a blackjack or gives me a karate chop to the neck—and the hammer slips out from under my nerveless thumb? I think the matter deserves our most careful consideration, don't you?"

There was a space of complete silence. The big man behind me, belatedly aware of the situation, had stopped moving. Dr. Perry licked his lips, watching the gun with fascination.

I said, "There is a time element involved, of course. It's quite a strain, holding a gun like this. When my thumb gets tired, and maybe a little slippery with sweat—Don't forget, I'm the guy whose hand keeps slipping and killing people."

"Eric," he said. "Eric, don't be hasty. I can understand the resentment you feel towards me, but I swear the instructions I gave you seemed perfectly safe, well within the bounds of what the subject could tolerate—"

I laughed. "Doctor, you flatter yourself. I'm not mad at you, although I do think you might at least wait for the autopsy results before talking as if it were all my fault. After all, you had a hand in it, too. But the hell with that. I'm not pointing a gun at you for personal reasons."

"Then what—"

I said, "You got a call from Washington while you were driving here, didn't you? You were told that my attitude seemed to be somewhat uncertain, and that it might be a good idea to make absolutely sure that I came in as ordered. Am I correct?"

He hesitated. Then he nodded reluctantly.

"All right," I said. "Well, here's a message to take back. Tell the man upstairs that limited measures have failed and the full mad-dog treatment may be indicated. Tell him that I recommend a silenced rifle with a telescopic sight. A shotgun could do the job, but it would be pretty damn noisy and messy. A good man with a pistol might deliver, but he'd be taking chances. I may have a superman complex, Doctor, but I'm not laboring under the delusion that I'm bullet-proof."

"Eric, you're talking wildly—"

"Shut up," I said, "and listen carefully. The one thing I want you to impress on him is that he must not make the mistake of trying to take me alive a second time. You're getting away with it tonight. No one else will. Do you understand? I may not be the best man he's got, but I'm pretty damn good; plenty good enough to handle anybody he sends after me with orders not to kill. Tell him not to waste trained men by ordering out to get me handicapped by silly instructions like that. They simply won't come back. Is that clear?"

Perry licked his lips again, watching the cocked revolver in my hand. "It's clear."

"I've been a member of this organization a long time, off and on," I said. "I know how it works. I know that if he really wants me, he can get me—dead. I'll even make it easy for him. I'm sticking to my cover as Lash Petroni, hoodlum. If I'm mowed down one dark night, it'll just go down in the records as another syndicate kill. If that's what he wants, tell him to go ahead. I won't even duck. I've got other things to do besides watching the bushes for hidden guns."

Perry asked quickly, "Other things? What other things do you have to do, Eric?"

"Never mind," I said. "He'll know. Just tell him the choice. He can have me killed. That's all he can do without risking a massacre that'll hit front pages clear across the country. I won't stand still for the dog-catcher with the net. I won't stand still for interference of any kind. If I bump into one of the boys, I'll go for him without asking questions. A savage battle to the death between agents of a super-secret government organization wouldn't look very nice in the headlines, would it? The publicity would put him out of business, and he knows it. And it's just what I'll give him if he tries any more of this horsing around. Tell him to send out the elimination squads or forget it. I'll be in touch when I have something to report."

"Eric," Perry said, "Eric, I want you to consider carefully the consequences of—"

"Never mind the consequences," I said. "He'll know what I'm doing and why I'm doing it. If he wants it done, tell him, leave me alone. If he doesn't, shoot me. That's his choice. And now you can tell your driver to get your patient the hell out of my car, but don't you move until I give the word—"

It was a tricky business, but not as bad as it might have been. He was just an expert on medical matters; I didn't have to worry about him. Pretty boy Alan wouldn't have worried me under any circumstances, certainly not with his mind on his tummy. The driver was my only real concern. He was probably an old pro, but I gave him no chance to prove it. While he was helping the walking wounded from one car to the other, I stepped into the little Ford and took off.

The mirror showed me an argument behind me. The driver obviously wanted to drop everything and come after me. In a 3.8 Jag sedan he could have run circles around what I was driving. But Dr. Perry had sworn an oath to Aesculapius, and his primary concern, after all, was Alan, not me. When last seen, they were loading the patient carefully into the imported sedan with the buggy-whip antenna.

Driving away, I tried to guess what Mac would do when he got my message. He'd get mad, of course, but that didn't matter; he wasn't a man to let temper affect his course of action. On the other hand, if he really thought I'd flipped and was an active menace—Come to think of it, I had been kind of casual about slipping that knife into Alan without even waiting for identification.

I shook my head quickly. Whether my brain was running smoothly on six cylinders or limping along on five, it was all the brain I had available. And there's a kind of unwritten rule in the organization that goes: *nobody dies for nothing*. It doesn't apply to sentimental schnooks like Alan, who get perforated making like damn fools on their own time. But Jean had been on duty when she died, grimly sticking out a lousy assignment.

And I'd been there. *She's got to survive, of course*, Mac had said. Those had been my orders. Exactly why she had died wasn't very important, in this connection. It had been my job to see that she didn't. The least I could do was take over where she'd left off, so her death wouldn't be, let's say, wasted.

It was very quiet at the Tidewater Motel when I reached it. The pool was deserted again. The water still looked blue-green and cold. The window of unit seventeen was dark. I knocked softly. The light came on, footsteps approached the door and it opened to show me the small face of Teddy Michaelis, yawning.

"You took long enough," she said. "Come in."

9

She was a pajama girl, which, if I'd come for pleasure instead of business, I'd have found disappointing: nighties are much nicer. With her short, blonde hair, in her loose blue-flowered silk coat and tapering blue trousers, she looked like a small, sleepy, barefoot boy.

"Well, get inside before somebody sees you, stupid," she snapped when I didn't move at once. I moved past her. She closed the door and locked it, saying, "I hope you had sense enough to make sure you weren't followed."

The room had unpleasant associations for me. It was almost an exact duplicate of Jean's, a few doors down. There was the same beige wall-to-wall carpet, the same blond furniture, and the same TV set on the same revolving stand. Only the feminine debris was different; Teddy Michaelis would never take any prizes for immaculate housekeeping, either.

I walked to the closet and looked inside. I inspected the bathroom and found it empty. I turned to look at the

small, boyish figure standing by the door, watching me
warily. Despite the aggressive attitude with which she'd
greeted me, she was obviously scared. I could hardly
blame her. From her point of view, it must have been kind
of like inviting a man-eating tiger to tea.

"Let's not play cowboys and Indians, doll," I said.
"Every cop in the state knows my car after the alarm
that went out. What was I supposed to do, take it out in
the woods and paint it pink, just for you?" She looked
disconcerted, and I went on, "As far as I know, I came
here clean. But I'm not guaranteeing how long it will last."

"Oh."

"Now," I said, "say something that makes it worth my
trouble." I glanced around once more, and decided to
take a chance on a mike. It didn't seem likely, under the
circumstances, that she was in league with the police; and
if anybody else was setting traps for me, I might as well
take the bait and see what happened next. "Let's start with
why you lied to the cops for me, doll," I said.

"Don't call me that."

I made her a sweeping bow. "I humbly apologize for
the familiarity, Miss Michaelis, ma'am."

"Papa used to call me doll," she said, still standing there
watching me, unmoving. "That's why—" She stopped.

"That's why you don't want to hear it from my
degenerate lips?"

She smiled slowly. She was gaining confidence, I saw.
She hadn't known just what to expect when I first came
in: a hoodlum, a murderer. Now she was realizing that,

depraved and wicked though Petroni might be, he was fundamentally just another male.

"You said that," she murmured. "I didn't."

"Your meaning got through, honey," I said. "Loud and clear. Any objection to honey?"

Her smile remained. "If you have to call me something, why not try Teddy?"

"Teddy," I said. "Like in bear. Okay, Teddy." I frowned at her. "So Papa used to call you doll?" She nodded. I said, "And Papa is Dr. Norman Michaelis, scientist, electronics expert, and Washington big-shot. Widower. One daughter and a private income from his inventions. I like that private income, Teddy. Folks with private incomes can afford to pay for their notions, even the crazy ones. What's your notion in getting me out of jail and asking me here?"

She didn't answer the direct question. She was frowning right back at me. "You checked up on me?"

"Did you think I wouldn't? A mouse I've never seen before saves me from the cops and asks me to a conference in her motel room. Would I walk in cold?"

She hesitated, and asked curiously, "What's a mouse, Jim?"

"Don't act dumb. A mouse is a broad."

"I mean," she persisted, "is it good or bad? Like dream-boat? Or like bitch?"

"A mouse," I said, "is something small and cuddly. Like a doll, which is what your daddy used to call you. Let's stick with that. Let's brush it hard and see where the dandruff falls. Used to? What made him stop?" She looked at me and didn't answer. I said, as if quoting from memory, which I was, "Dr. Norman Michaelis is currently resting and relaxing aboard a seagoing yacht belonging to friends. That's the official scoop. Don't ask me how I got it. I've got connections."

Actually, I'd got it from the dope given me by Mac during the preliminary briefing. Michaelis' disappearance had been temporarily covered up, to avoid embarrassing questions while the search was in progress.

The little girl said quickly, "It isn't true. I suppose they mean the *Freya*, but she's anchored up a creek not twenty miles from here, where she can't be seen unless you're right on top of her. Nobody's aboard except Nick, the paid hand. They've painted out the name and home port, but how many jib-headed, eighty-foot schooners are there on the Bay? I got that much for my money, anyway, before somebody got to the man I'd hired and bought him off. Or scared him off. Anyway, he turned in one report and quit."

I said, "You're throwing it at me fast. Is it supposed to make sense? What's a jib-headed schooner?"

"A schooner is a two-masted sailing vessel, fore-and-aft rigged, with the taller mast aft. If it has a Marconi mainsail, it's jib-headed. Because it comes to a point at the top like a jib, get it? Or do I have to tell you what a jib is, Jim?"

I hadn't reacted the first time she used my name, so this time she called attention to it with a little smile; she was treating me just like a human being. She wasn't scared a bit, even if I did go around killing people, her smile said. She found a cigarette on the dresser, lit it, and sat down on the bed facing me, smoking bravely.

"The jib's the little triangular sail up front. I know that much," I said. "And Freya was the Norse goddess of love and beauty. And an eighty-footer is a lot of boat, for a private yacht. And who did you hire to do what, Teddy?"

"A private detective from a New York agency. I've been working in New York. When Papa disappeared—"

"Disappeared?"

"His letters stopped coming. I called his lab in Washington and they said he was taking a vacation, but he hadn't written me anything about it. They said he'd come down here. They sounded—well, funny. So I called *her* long distance—"

"Who?"

"You know. You met her. The horsy aristocratic lady with the sharp, sharp eye."

"Mrs. Rosten?"

Teddy nodded. "And she said he was off cruising somewhere, like you just told me. She'd lent him the schooner, she said."

"I see. Well, I wish I had a handsome lady friend who lent me eighty-foot yachts. So your daddy used to call you doll, but he doesn't any more, because he's off cruising the seven seas in a schooner that's tied up in a creek twenty miles from here with the name painted out. And you sent a New York private eye to investigate, and he came back with his tail between his legs. And just where the hell does this Rosten dame come into the act, anyway?"

Teddy hesitated. "Papa—well, Papa was crazy about her," she said reluctantly.

"Tsk, tsk," I said. "A married woman? How did she feel about it?"

"Feel?" There was sudden viciousness in the little girl's voice. "What makes you think she's got feelings, that female vampire? Don't flatter her, Jim!"

"In other words," I said, "you don't like her very much."

"She's a monster!" the girl said fiercely. "Who was that ancient character who turned men into swine?"

"Circe, I think," I said. "She wasn't ancient at the time, as I recall."

"Well, this one is," Teddy said. "God, she must be almost forty, and she had Papa making a fool of himself like they were both kids in their teens!"

"Think of it," I said, "an old hag like that. Almost forty!"

She glanced up quickly. I don't exactly qualify as a dewy juvenile myself. She had the grace to look embarrassed.

"I didn't mean—anyway, it's different with a man."

"Sure. Men age better."

"Well, they do. I—I just couldn't understand it. What he saw in her, I mean. It wasn't as if she were pretty or anything, or even very bright. I mean, all she can talk about is horses and dogs and boats, real sexy conversation. The only thing I can figure is, she must be good in bed, but she doesn't look it."

I said, "And you don't like the idea of her being good in bed with your papa, anyway."

"Well, should I?" she snapped. "I tried to tell him, to warn him. Somebody had to tell him he was making himself utterly ridiculous! We had a terrible fight about it, and I packed my things and moved to New York and said I wasn't going to set foot in the house again until he'd made a clean break with that woman."

"That's known as polite blackmail," I said. "Impolite blackmail is when you ask for money."

She flushed. "I had to do something! I couldn't just stand by and let him ruin everything. I didn't even answer his letters. He made me so mad! He kept writing to me as if I were a child who just didn't understand. I understood, all right. I just thought it was disgusting!" She drew a long, ragged breath. "And now—and now he's gone." She paused. "I think he's dead, Jim. Murdered!"

"Murdered?"

"Yes, and it's her fault. I know it is!"

"Mrs. Rosten? Why would she kill him?"

"I didn't say she killed him. I said it was her fault." Teddy glanced at me, somewhat hesitantly, and went on, "I think—I think her husband killed him in a fit of jealousy. Don't laugh. That's the way it must have happened!" She drew on her cigarette defiantly.

I studied her for a moment. I was realizing, rather

belatedly, that I was dealing with a screwball. It changed the situation somewhat.

"I'm not laughing," I said. "I'm just panting, trying to catch up. You're leaving me way behind."

She said, "Well, it's logical, isn't it? She's beat on that poor man for years. He's definitely unstable, anyway. Anybody can see that. She's flaunted her lovers in his face, time and again. Everybody knows it around here. I think it finally just got too much for him and he went off his trolley."

"Have you got any evidence for all this?" I asked. "Or are you making it up as you go along? Half freshman psychology and half TV?"

She said, "Well, if Papa isn't dead, where is he? I think there was a dreadful scene of some kind, and Louis Rosten went haywire and killed him. Then she helped her husband cover up to avoid the scandal of a murder trial that would have crucified her. Why is the *Freya* hidden in that creek? Why is Louis absolutely terrified of his wife? Why did that private detective drop the case after coming down here? She either bought him off or threatened him with political influence; her family's been big stuff in this state since Lord Calvert founded Baltimore."

"Lord who?" I asked.

"Calvert," she said. "They pronounce it Caulvert around here."

"So you came down to get the goods on her?"

"What else could I do?" Teddy shrugged her small shoulders under the silk pajama coat. "I hoped they'd invite me to stay at the house out on Long Point, but I guess they knew I meant trouble. They gave me some story about remodeling the guest wing and got me a room here. Then they had me to dinner with this creepy Thunderbird character. One of them was watching me every minute I was in the house, either Louis or her, and I wasn't too sure about Thunderbird. He's some kind of relative. And then we came back here to go swimming—swimming, with the temperature nudging absolute zero! They just had to dream up some excuse to get me out of there and back to the motel."

"And you saw me," I said, "and after you'd learned who I was, it came to you in a flash that I was just what you needed, even if you had to lie like a trooper to get me."

"Yes," she said. "Of course. There wasn't any point in trying another private detective; she'd have got to him, too."

"So what can Lash Petroni do for you that a private dick can't?"

"The police said you were a hoodlum, a gangster. You don't talk like a hoodlum. Not all the time, anyway."

I chided myself for being careless, and put on a grin. "What's the matter, small stuff? Just because I happen to know that Freya was the goddess of love and Circe turned men into swine—ain't it allowed for us criminal classes to read a book between hits?"

She flushed. "I didn't mean—what's a hit?"

"A hit," I said, "is like when you're sent to take care of somebody who's bothering somebody, and that's enough stalling around, pint-size. You pried me loose from the fuzz; you got me here. Now tell me what the hell you want and what's in it for mc, or I'll be on my way."

She hesitated, still watching me closely. Then she crushed out her cigarette, got to her feet and came forward, taking my lapels between her thumbs and forefingers. She looked up. Her eyes were very blue and bright in her small face. When she spoke, her voice sounded kind of shaky and breathless.

"I want—" She paused, then went on, "How much would you charge to make a hit for me, Jim Petroni?"

10

I paused outside the door and fingered the bills in my pocket and wondered if I was giving the little girl a great big bargain or overcharging her outrageously. I wasn't up on current prices; Mac had neglected to tell me what Lash Petroni was supposed to charge for his services. I guess it hadn't occurred to him that employment might actually be offered me under this name.

I shook my head, squared my snappy, narrow-brimmed dark hat on my head, settled my sharp, narrow-shouldered dark coat, and headed for the car. When I got where I could see it plainly, I stopped. A man was sitting in the front seat, waiting for me.

I stood there for quite a while, feeling hurt and disappointed. I mean, I'd made myself perfectly clear. I'd said, *If I bump into one of the boys, I'll go for him without asking questions.*

It was too bad all around. It may have been a silly thing to say, but in the business we don't send messages like that without intending to back them up, regardless of consequences. Mac should have known I wouldn't try to bluff him. I reached slowly for Alan's revolver, for the second time that night. I moved to a corner of the building that would give me a rest for my gun hand. You can generally get by with one shot at that hour of the night, even a loud one from a short-barreled .38 Special. People will stir in their beds, they may even sit up and listen, but if they hear nothing more, it's a good bet they won't bother to rise and investigate.

I checked the line of fire carefully. There was nothing to deflect the bullet on my side of the target. Beyond, there was no risk of disabling my car if I got total penetration— not likely with a head shot at that range, anyway—and what happened to other cars down the row wasn't any worry. I drew back the hammer to full cock, and settled the rectangular blade of the front sight into the square notch of the rear sight. As I did so, the man in the car turned his head impatiently and looked back towards the building, obviously wondering what the hell was keeping me so long.

I let my pent-up breath go out slowly, and eased the pressure on the trigger. I was looking over the sights of a loaded and cocked revolver at the plump, cheerful features of Mr. William Orcutt, of the Annapolis Orcutts, known variously as Billy and Thunderbird.

I was shaking a little as I put the gun away. I walked quickly over there. He opened the car door as I came up.

"Mr. Petroni—"

I grabbed him by the coat and hauled him out. "What the hell are you doing in my car?"

"I wanted to talk with you, Mr. Petroni." He freed himself and smoothed his rumpled coat. "I wanted to tell you—"

He stopped, obviously embarrassed about something, trying to find the right words. I studied him bleakly. He wasn't bad-looking, just a little softer and heavier than he should have been—a crew-cut baby-face. Swimming was the only sport he'd be really good at, with that figure, but it wasn't the figure I was worrying about. I kept seeing his head the way it would have looked with a bullet-hole in it.

"What did you want to tell me, punk?" My harsh voice didn't sound quite right, even for hard-boiled Petroni.

"I wanted, well, to tell you to stay way from Miss Michaelis." He hesitated, but I didn't say anything, and he went on quickly, "She's—well, a little mixed up. She told me, well, never mind. She's got some weird ideas. But I don't want you taking advantage of—I mean, she's a lovely person, but she needs someone to look after her."

"And you've elected yourself to the job?"

He cleared his throat, a little self-consciously. "Well, yes. After the way she insisted on waiting to speak with you outside the police station, it was obvious she had something crazy in mind. I—" He stopped and squared his shoulders. "I don't intend to let her ruin her life by becoming involved with a racketeer and strong-arm man, Mr. Petroni. She's just a crazy kid; she doesn't mean everything she says. I think she likes to pretend. Stay away from her, Petroni."

"Yeah," I said. "Stay away from her. Sure."

I hit him. I gave it to him hard and low, without warning, and he went to the ground, hugging himself where it hurt; and somebody was coming at me from behind. I whirled, ready, but it was only Teddy Michaelis in her blue pajamas. She made her way up to us cautiously, still barefooted, and looked down. Orcutt pushed himself to hands and knees, retching painfully.

"What did you do that for?" Teddy asked me. There was no reproach in her voice, only curiosity.

"I felt like it," I said. I didn't say I'd hit him because I'd come damn close to killing him. She wouldn't have understood. I wasn't sure I understood myself.

She giggled. "He looks awfully silly, doesn't he? Poor boy. I heard what he said. I think it's kind of cute, his wanting to protect me, don't you?"

"Yeah, cute," I said. "When he catches his breath, clean him up and send him home. I'll call you tomorrow. Good night."

As I drove away, I kept hearing Mac's voice in my head: *I have seen it happen before in men whose occupation allows them to kill and get away with it.* I'd laughed at the time, but now I had to face the fact that twice in one night I'd almost killed a man, quite casually, without even making sure of his identity first. *After a while,* Mac had said, *their judgment becomes impaired, since human life has ceased to have much value for them.*

I'd almost killed two men, and I had killed a woman. At least Jean had died, and I was no longer so sure that my hand hadn't slipped, a little. Maybe I'd even wanted it to slip, as Mac had said, subconsciously...

I found a hotel, got a room, and sent the bellboy away with a tip. I opened the suitcase he'd placed on the stand at the foot of the bed and grimaced at the gaudy Petroni apparel inside. I found a silver flask and started towards the bathroom for a glass and said to hell with it. Drinking when I felt lousy had never made me feel any better. I screwed the cap back onto the flask and dropped the flask back into the suitcase. The telephone rang. I picked it up.

"Is this Mr. Peterson?" a female voice asked. "Is this Mr. Peterson, from Chicago?"

"I'm sorry," I said. "I'm from Chicago, but the name is Peters, ma'am. James A. Peters."

"Oh, dear," the voice said. "I'm terribly sorry. I do hope I didn't wake you, or anything."

"It's perfectly all right, ma'am," I said.

I put the instrument back in its cradle. It was code, of course. There were half a dozen names she might have asked for. Peterson meant I was supposed to hunt up a clear phone and call Washington. I didn't ask myself how Mac had known where to reach me. After all, I'd told him I had a date with the Michaelis kid, whose temporary residence was known; and I hadn't made it very hard for anybody who wanted to tail me from there. The only question was, should I call and learn where I stood, or should I be proud and independent.

I didn't feel very proud and independent. I went down into the lobby and used one of the pay phones.

"Eric here," I said, when I heard the familiar voice on the line.

Mac said, "Yellow Cadillac two-door, male driver."

"It rings no bells."

"It should. He was behind you all the way from the girl's motel, our man says, trying to make up his mind to close in. No armaments in view, but that means nothing."

"No, sir."

"I got your message."

"Yes, sir."

"Independence is a virtue, I'm told, but there are arguments in favor of discipline. We will discuss the matter later."

"Yes, sir."

"I presume what you have in mind could be classified under the heading of atonement. Even assuming that you were at fault, which you have denied, it is a sentimental notion."

"Yes, sir."

"Sentiment is rare in our line of work." His voice was dry. "Well, Jean would have appreciated the romantic gesture. Since you seem to have a lead of sorts and nobody else has, you may as well carry on, if you feel capable—What did you say?"

"Nothing," I said. "Nothing at all, sir."

"What did the little Michaelis girl have to propose?"

"She has hired me to assassinate Mrs. Louis Rosten in a discreet way. Twenty-five hundred down, twenty-five hundred on delivery. I've only collected five C's so far, but

I'm getting the rest tomorrow after she's been to the bank."

It silenced him briefly. I'd hoped it might. He asked at last, "What are your plans?"

I said, "I thought the deal was that no questions would be asked."

"That was in another connection. You can't very well—"

"Can't I?" I asked. "How important is this machine of Dr. Michaelis'? The last I heard, the fate of the world hung in the balance."

"But—" I heard him swallow at the other end of the line. He thought I was needling him, but he wasn't quite sure. Well, I wasn't quite sure, either. He called my bluff. "Very well. Use your judgment."

"Thank you, sir, but judgment-wise I'm suffering from fatigue, remember? And a superman complex. Ah, hell." I was being childish. "I want everything anybody's got on Michaelis, Theodora. Orcutt, William. Rosten, Robin. Rosten, Louis. And a schooner named *Freya*. Oh, and a man named Nick, paid hand on the schooner. Can do?"

"I think we have most of that information. In a minute, I'll switch you to the girl downstairs and she'll read it off for you. Anything else?"

"One thing. There was a New York private detective, name unknown, who came down here to investigate for Miss Michaelis and got scared off."

"He was taken aside by some people with impressive credentials and told to forget it."

"That wasn't too smart," I said. "It would have been

better, maybe, to let him keep working and have him send her innocuous reports, or maybe not. This way the little girl's on the warpath. Maybe she'll help us blast something loose."

"Yes. It would be well, however, if the blast damage were confined to a reasonable area. Eric?"

"Yes, sir?"

"Concerning Michaelis, senior. Keep in mind that this is a valuable man. Merely because the orders permit a certain course of action does not imply that course is mandatory. I had some high officials in here this evening—"

I said, "Do they want him shut up or don't they? This isn't the search-and-rescue branch of the U.S. Coast Guard, for God's sake! There's only one chance in a thousand I can even reach the guy, and if I do, I may have all of ten seconds to act. Now, do I have the go-ahead or don't I?"

He sighed. "You have it."

I hesitated. "How's Alan, sir?"

"Alan is going to be all right."

"Sure," I said. "Well, give me that office girl and let me find out something about these people. A yellow Cadillac, you say?"

"That's right. Be careful. Report when you can." He paused. "As for that matter of discipline—"

"Sir?"

"It will depend on which of us turns out to be right, won't it, Eric?" He cleared his throat delicately. "Judgment-wise, I mean."

11

When I came out of the hotel, after getting the information I wanted, the sky to the east held a pale hint of dawn. There weren't any yellow Cadillacs around. I hoped I hadn't lost him. I started walking. It might not be the best plan, judgment-wise, but I was too sleepy to be clever. I wanted to stir up some action, and if it happened to involve hand grenades, submachine-guns, or sawed-off shotguns, well, it was about time a little hardware came my way, for a change, so I could prove I could be real tough on the receiving end, too.

Atonement, Mac had said. He'd pulled the rug out from under me very neatly—or, rather, instead of pulling it out, he'd left me standing on it. He'd given me no chance to back away from the position I'd chosen. To put it a different way, I'd stuck my neck way out, with melodramatic flourishes, and instead of crudely chopping it off, as I'd invited him to do, he'd just pulled it out a little farther and tied a pink ribbon around it...

Balanced or unbalanced, glad or sorry, I was stuck with the job. In theory, I was picking up the case where Jean had left it. In practice, I wasn't anywhere near that place and had no idea where to find it. Jean, according to her reports, had had a real contact, a muffled voice on the phone, somebody interested enough in an alcoholic, disillusioned, potentially disloyal member of our team to make propositions; interested enough to bug her motel room and check up on her. All I had, so far, was a screwy kid with a grudge against her vanished papa's handsome lady friend.

What I needed was action, I thought, or about twelve hours' sleep, or a month in the sun with a lady named Gail. Well, it was no time to start thinking about that. I was thinking about it, nevertheless, when a yellow Cadillac glided up beside me and stopped. I stopped. The near door of the car opened, and the handsome, sunburned face of Louis Rosten looked out.

"Please get in, Mr. Petroni," Rosten said. "I've been trying to catch you. I would like to speak with you."

I shrugged and got in. He sent the car away smoothly. Well, it was action of a sort. I leaned against the door, watching him drive and wondering if he could possibly be Jean's mysterious telephone contact. That slick, gutless air could be a fake—so could Orcutt's Don Quixote act. So could Mrs. Rosten's air of regal indifference, or pretty little Teddy Michaelis' pose of a bloodthirsty kitten.

"I'll buy you a cup of coffee," Rosten said. "We'll drive out the highway. Under the circumstances, I think it is better if we're not recognized eating together, don't you?"

I shrugged. "Circumstances? What circumstances? I've got nothing to hide."

"Nothing except a murder," Rosten said.

It was hard to think of Jean's death in those terms; but of course Petroni would. "What are you driving at, mister?" I demanded with sudden harshness. "The cops let me go, didn't they?"

"Please!" he said. "Don't think I have any intention of—what I mean is, Petroni, I do have eyes in my head, whatever my wife may think. You're rather a distinctive figure. I could have made a great deal of trouble for you last night, but I chose not to. That's all I'm trying to say."

I studied him balefully. "Okay," I said. "Okay, so you saw me and kept quiet. What do you figure it's going to buy you? What do you think you've got on me? You'd play hell trying to change your story now. The police would crucify you."

"Please," he said. "I'm not a blackmailer. I have no intention of changing my testimony. The dead woman was nothing to me; nor do I have any strong feelings about law and order. I must say, however, that I am curious. How did you get Miss Michaelis to lie for you, too? Had you known her before?"

I said, "She's my long-lost kid sister. It was a family reunion. How could she send me to the electric chair, her own flesh and blood?"

He glanced at me, and laughed politely to show he got the joke. "Ha ha. Well, never mind. It isn't important, except that it enabled me to find you again. Knowing that she'd lied for you, I could guess that you would make contact with her sooner or later. It was merely a matter of—well, of getting away from my wife unsuspected, so I could watch the motel. Of course I couldn't let *her* know what I was doing."

"Of course not," I said. "She might have got the wrong idea about your hanging around a pretty young girl."

He looked a little startled, as if I'd offered an unexpected thought. Then he laughed again, rather nervously. "Ha ha. Yes, well, there's that, too. And of course Teddy, Miss Michaelis, is quite attractive. There's something very charming about a small, really feminine woman, don't you think?"

I had a picture in my mind of the small, really feminine woman asking bright-eyed, *How much would you charge to make a hit for me?* But it wasn't for me to disillusion him, if he wanted to take her doll-like appearance at face value.

"Feeling that way," I said, "maybe you should have married one."

"Maybe I should."

"Of course," I said, "there's something even more charming about a rich woman."

He laughed. "If you're trying to insult me, Petroni, you're wasting your time. Of course my wife is wealthy. Of course I married her for her wealth—why else would anyone marry such a female horse?"

"I think Mrs. Rosten is quite a handsome dame, myself."

"Handsome!" he said. "My God, man, do you know what it's like, living with a handsome woman with the authority of money behind her, and a will of iron?"

"No," I said. "I don't know what it's like. I never had any offers."

"I'm a sensitive man," he said. "I—I feel things. She has no conception of—she is a brutal woman, Petroni. A horrible woman, a grasping, selfish, avaricious woman. She has a pathological sense of family and property. She shot a child once, a mere boy, who'd broken into the house at night and was making away with a silver candlestick. I watched her throw the shells into that Purdey shotgun of hers—she loves to hunt—and close the breech deliberately and take aim out the window, swinging the gun as casually as if she were knocking over a rabbit. When we got out there, the boy was dead. The buckshot had practically torn him to shreds. It was dreadful!"

"I always figure a burglar takes his chances like anybody else outside the law. Your wife sounds like quite a girl."

"You'd say that. I don't suppose a human life means anything to you, either."

It was an echo of what Mac had said, and I didn't like Rosten any better for saying it, even though he was saying it to Lash Petroni, not Matt Helm.

"Well, no little juvenile slob had better try running off with any of my silver, mister. If I had any. What did Mrs. Rosten have to say about it?"

Rosten grimaced. "She said, 'I couldn't let him get

away with great-grandmother Sandeman's candlestick, could I?'"

"Did she get away with it?" I asked. "I guess she must have. She isn't in jail."

"Of course she got away with it," he said resentfully. "She always does, no matter what high-handed action it may be. Well, not quite always. There was the time she tried to hold off the Federal Government with that same Purdey double—they were taking over some run-down family property she'd inherited down the Bay. For the Navy, I think. They talked her out of it, somehow. I think they just made her see she was making herself perfectly ridiculous, and there's nothing she hates worse than that. Well, here we are." He stopped the big car at a roadside joint, half restaurant, half drive-in. "We might as well have our coffee in the car," he said.

"Sure."

I told the girl who came up that I'd have coffee and a doughnut. He ordered black coffee and watched the girl move away through the lights in tight lavender pants and a frilly white blouse. At that angle, retreating, the pants were much more interesting than the blouse. Rosten licked his lips thoughtfully.

"I—I have a proposition for you, Petroni," he said.

"I know," I said. "It'll cost you five grand. Twenty-five hundred down, twenty-five hundred on delivery. Cash. No bills larger than a hundred; I like fifties and twenties better."

He turned sharply to stare at me, shocked that I'd read

his mind. From his expression, I knew I'd read it right. Before he had recovered, the girl was returning. From this angle, advancing, the blouse was more interesting than the pants, but the poor guy wasn't noticing.

"I'll take the coffee with cream, miss," I said, and waited until she'd gone. "Get to the bank as soon as it opens," I said, to Rosten. "Well, there's no rush; any time today will do. Twenty-five hundred in used bills. You know the countryside; you pick a place where we can get together this evening. After dark would be best. I don't have to tell you to keep an eye on the rearview mirror. We don't want any witnesses to this little transaction, do we, mister?"

He watched me take a bite of doughnut as if he'd never seen a man eat before. He licked his lips. "I—I don't know what you're talking about," he said weakly. "I don't— there must be some misunderstanding. I didn't—"

I said, "What's the matter, is the price too steep for you? Hell, you're making a million on the deal; what's five grand to you?"

"A million!" He cleared his throat and said more strongly, "Really, Mr. Petroni, I'm afraid we're talking at cross purposes. The proposition I had in mind—"

"Was killing your wife," I said.

He turned pale and looked around fearfully. I thought he'd actually put his fingers to his lips and say hush. He started to speak, but nothing came.

"Cut it out, little man," I said. "Last night you lied for me. Why? Why did you help me stay out of jail, knowing

I was a murderer? This morning you went to a lot of trouble to find me—and to make sure your wife didn't know you were trying to find me. Why? You've told me you married her only for her money. You've told me what a terrible person she is. Hell, she's a murderer herself, according to you; she deserves to die. That's what you were saying just now, isn't it? You were trying to justify what you were going to ask me to do to her. What the hell did you look me up for, if not to have me kill her? I don't do plumbing or paint houses or wash cars, mister. The police told you what my business is."

I sounded as if I'd figured it out very logically. I didn't bother to tell him I'd been able to guess what was in his mind because somebody else had already introduced me to the same idea. A coincidence? Maybe, but if you leave a loaded gun lying around, it's apt to give ideas to more than one person. To these folks, I was just that: a deadly weapon provided in the hour of need by, so they thought, a benevolent fortune.

Rosten still hadn't spoken. I said, "Okay, so it's settled. Where's a good place for us to meet?"

He licked his lips. "Well," he said, "well, there's a place down on the Bay, a little cove called Mason's Cove—"

"Show me on the map, if you've got a map." He had one. He showed me. I asked, "When can you be there with the money?"

"I—we're going out this evening. A cocktail party at the Sandemans'. I don't know if I can get away afterwards."

"You'd better get away, mister. I don't work for

nothing. What about before the party? We'll take a chance on daylight."

"All right." His tongue came out again and discovered that his lips were still there. "All right. Four-thirty at the cove. Don't drive too far down that side road or you'll get stuck in the sand—Petroni?"

"Yes?"

"It will—" He did the tongue bit once more. "It will look like an accident, won't it?"

I said, "One day I'm going to have somebody ask me to do a murder that looks like a murder—"

He drove me back into town and dropped me a couple of blocks from the hotel. I watched the big car drive away. Then I found a phone booth in a drugstore, looked up a number in the book, and dialed it. A maid answered.

"I'd like to speak with Mrs. Rosten," I said. "Mrs. Louis Rosten. This is Jim Peters. She'll remember me."

"Mrs. Rosten's asleep, sir."

"Wake her up," I said. "It's important."

I waited. Presently I heard the maid return and pick up the phone. "Mr. Peters?"

"Yes," I said.

Her voice sounded a little breathless. "Miz Rosten say she sure do remember you, Mr. Peters, and she can't think of a thing she have to say to you this hour of the morning or any hour. She say, if you bother her again, she call the police!"

"I see," I said. "Thank you."

I hung up. Well, I wouldn't really have known how

to handle it if the woman had come to the phone, but I'd had to make at least a gesture towards playing it straight, like a conscientious government agent who'd stumbled on a dark conspiracy against a citizen's life—two dark conspiracies, to be exact.

12

I spent the rest of the morning catching up on my sleep. After lunch, I called Teddy Michaelis at the motel and arranged to meet her at a town called St. Alice. It was twenty miles from Annapolis, according to the map, but only ten from the cove where I was supposed to meet Rosten, later. I didn't give that as a reason for selecting it as a rendezvous, however.

I'd picked the town, but she, knowing the area a little better, had picked the meeting place: a bar and seafood joint built on a long pier sticking out over the water. The ceilings were low, the light was poor, the floor linoleum was cracked, and the tables had gingham tablecloths that could have been cleaner, but the bar was quite handsome: a great, massive, old-fashioned hunk of mahogany.

I was nursing a beer, taking it easy, when Teddy came in, carrying a folded newspaper under her arm. She was wearing snug white pants and a blue sweater with a hood, thrown back casually from her blonde head. Her mouth was as grim as such a small mouth could be, and her blue eyes were bright and angry. She came right over to the bar.

"What'll you have?" I asked.

"It isn't true!" she said fiercely.

"Simmer down, small stuff," I said. "I asked you a question. What'll you have?"

"It isn't true! Papa would never dream of—"

"I'll ask you once more. If I don't get a straight answer, I'll walk out on you. What'll you have?"

"But—oh, all right, damn you! Get me a—a bourbon on the rocks."

"Bourbon on the rocks for the lady," I told the barman. "Another beer for me. We'll take them in one of the booths."

I took Teddy by the arm, marched her across the room and set her down in one of the dark booths that lined the far wall. She slapped the paper down on the gingham tablecloth.

"It's a lousy lie!" she said.

"If you say so. What is?"

She shoved the paper towards me. I took it, opened it, and saw that the hurricane was gaining on us. Georgia was catching it now and the Carolinas were braced for the assault.

"Not there, stupid!" Teddy said. "The right-hand column. That damn reporter! That damn paper!"

I looked where she pointed. The column was headed: SCIENTIST MISSING. A quick glance through the text indicated that, like the New York private eye, a Washington reporter had stumbled on the interesting clue of the hidden schooner, as well as certain other facts, and had managed to worm an admission out of a certain government agency with which Michaelis had been connected. Murder, suicide and kidnaping were all considered, and while the reporter didn't actually say that Michaelis might have decamped under his own power, he did say that the agency in question categorically denied the possibility that Michaelis might have decamped under his own power.

"Don't you see what he's doing?" Teddy demanded. "He's giving the impression without saying a word—everybody who reads that will think Papa's a traitor! They're trying to cover up, that's what they're doing. Trying to make it look as if he disappeared voluntarily, so they won't have to embarrass the influential Mrs. Rosten!"

"I see," I said. "So you're still on the Rosten kick?"

She looked startled and indignant. "Why, yes, of course. That's what happened, you know it is. Why, it says right here in the paper they're the ones who found Papa's boat, she and Louis."

"They found it sailing along empty, according to the story," I pointed out.

She laughed scornfully. "Naturally they'd say that. They went out to look for him in the power cruiser, in the dark. They'd been drinking, probably; they hit the cocktails hard every evening. They found Papa, and there was a terrible drunken quarrel on the way back to shore—" She stopped, and swallowed something in her throat. "Afterwards—afterwards they had to say they found the boat empty. What else could they say?"

"Whatever they said, it seems to have convinced the police and the U.S. Government."

"Oh, I'm sure she was convincing as hell! She always is, with that damn great-lady act of hers. Offering to cooperate with the authorities in every respect, even to hiding the *Freya* to make it look as if Papa was off cruising. The longer the government held off announcing that he was missing, the safer she was, she and Louis. Well, she's not as safe as she thinks!" The kid looked at me across the gingham-covered table. "That is, if you haven't changed your mind, Petroni."

I shook my head. "Drink up and let's get out of here," I said.

Outside, we had to stop for a moment to get used to the sunlight. The front door faced a wide, reedy arm of Chesapeake Bay. The day was bright and, in contrast to the preceding night, quite warm, and people were sailing and fishing out there, forgetting the month's bills and the day's headlines. It seemed like a fine idea. I thought I'd have to try it some time.

"Okay, small stuff," I said, holding out my hand.

She fished a crumpled envelope out of her tight pants. I opened it and counted the bills inside. I closed it again and tucked it away in my coat. Teddy giggled and took my arm as we walked towards the shore.

"I like you, Jim," she said. "I had a dog once that was

just like you, a big black Doberman. He'd bite anybody
I told him to. I didn't even have to tell him. If I didn't
like them, I'd just snap my fingers and he'd go for them.
I taught him that. Papa thought he was just getting mean,
the way Dobermans do. Papa didn't know. The dog's
name was King. Papa had him put away, finally. I cried
all night, I was nine years old."

"Sure," I said. "Will you cry all night if they put me
away, Teddy?"

"Don't say that!" She stopped, swinging to face me. "I
don't want you to take any chances. I do like you. At least
you're honest, in a brutal sort of way. You don't pretend
to be something you aren't, like everybody else I know."

Even if she was a screwball, even if she had murder
on her twisted little mind, it made me feel a little guilty
to have her say that to me. Anyway, that was my first
reaction. And then I found myself wondering if maybe
that wasn't the reaction she'd been trying for.

It occurred to me suddenly that I'd been overlooking
something: I'd been overlooking the fact that Jean's room
had been wired for sound. She'd reported to that effect,
and an agent of her experience wouldn't make a mistake
about it. I had to assume, therefore, that some tapes had
been recorded last night. I had to assume that the person
I was trying to locate—the contact—had already played
those tapes, carefully studying the dialogue that had
passed between Jean and me before she died. I'd been
putting on an act of sorts, if you recall—so had Jean—
but anybody listening to our recorded conversation would

certainly know I wasn't a gangster named Petroni.

Yet the two people who had made contact with me so far had acted on the assumption that I really was Lash Petroni, a ruthless, unscrupulous, but possibly useful individual: a killer for hire. Or had they? It was, after all, a coincidence that two people should have hit on the idea of hiring me for the same job. Perhaps at least one of them knew perfectly well that the man he—or she—was ostensibly trying to bribe to commit murder was really a government agent. Perhaps it was a clever cover-up as well as a delicious joke and a way of keeping an eye on my activities…

I glanced at the kid standing in front of me with the sun bright on her cap of pale hair. Her words ran through my head again: *You don't pretend to be anything you aren't.* She could be perfectly sincere in her cockeyed way, but I couldn't overlook the possibility that she was throwing me a mocking hint, taunting me with her secret knowledge that, as a one-man Murder, Inc., I was the world's biggest fake.

I said, "Everybody pretends something, small fry. How are you at pretending?"

Her blue eyes got narrow, as if I'd accused her of something. Well, maybe I had. "Are you busy tonight?" I asked easily.

She relaxed. "Well, yes. I have a date."

"Break it. Wait a minute. Who's the guy?"

"Who would it be?" she asked with a grimace. "How many people do I really know in this forsaken town? He kept pestering me and what else was there to do except sit in that lousy motel room and think?"

"Orcutt?" I said. "Well, can you get him to take you to a cocktail party being given this evening by some people named Sandeman? I gather they're relatives of Mrs. Rosten, which means they're relatives of Orcutt, so he should be able to swing it."

She said, "Well, I can try, but—"

"When you get there," I said, "ditch the Thunderbird boy temporarily and make a play for Louis Rosten. Can you do that? Can you play them both, Orcutt and Rosten? Can you take Rosten away from his wife and make her mad so she'll march out of the place fuming—and then can you get the two men together and spend the evening with them? I think it would be a good idea if you all wound up at the Rosten place for drinks, say eleven–twelve o'clock. Can you swing that?"

She hesitated. Her eyes were bright, contemplating the challenge. "Of course I can, but—but why do you want me to do it?"

I said, "Don't be more stupid than you have to. I want Mrs. Rosten alone, naturally. And I think it would be a hell of a good idea if you had a solid alibi for the whole evening. Don't you?"

"Oh." Her breath caught. "I see. You mean—it's tonight? So soon?"

"Do you want me to stall around so you can dream about it?" I glanced at her, and said casually, "Talking about dreams, I forgot to ask what kind of a job you want me to do. Smooth or rough?"

She frowned. "What do you mean?"

I said impatiently, "Hell, the price you're paying entitles you to a few frills if you want them. So tell me, do you just want the dame dead? Or do you want her dead with her face smashed in, her teeth knocked out, her breasts sliced off, and her fingernails ripped out by the bloody roots?"

She gulped. "Don't be so damn graphic, Jim!"

I said sneeringly, "That's what I thought! You're really chicken, aren't you? Now you listen to me and get this straight: we don't give refunds. You can call it off now, but once we leave here you're in for the whole job and the whole five grand; so don't come whimpering to me later about how you've changed your mind." I took the envelope out of my pocket and held it out. "This is it, kid. In or out. You call it."

She hesitated. I let my lip curl scornfully. She saw it and slapped the envelope aside. "Go ahead," she said. "Go ahead, Jim! I'll be there; midnight at the Rosten house. And you can do it just as rough as you please; it can't be too rough for me!" She giggled abruptly.

"What's funny?"

"Just something you said. She'd never miss them."

"Miss what?"

"She's pretty flat-chested, you know. She'd never miss them."

I watched her run along the pier to the shore and jump into a small white sports car—an MG, if it matters. She clashed the gears badly getting into low, and again shifting up, which is hard to do with a synchromesh transmission, but she managed. She was really a pretty horrible little girl. At least she was working hard to give that impression.

13

I was early for Rosten. It's always best to beat the other party to the rendezvous if you don't trust him very much; besides, I wanted to look the place over and see if it would do for another purpose I had in mind. It was a pretty, sandy cove bordered by a honeysuckle jungle such as they have in this part of the world; anybody who thinks of that stuff as just a pretty garden vine has never been in Maryland. Presently the big yellow Cadillac came nosing through the tangled woods like a prehistoric monster, and stopped at the parking place favored by the people who used the beach for picnics in the summer. You could tell by the rusty beer cans.

I settled with Rosten quickly enough and had him drive me back to town, leaving my car where it was hidden. I gave him instructions paralleling those I'd given Teddy. He didn't like the idea of doing or knowing anything about it until I brought up the alibi question and pointed out the legal advantages of having people around at the moment of his great bereavement.

Later that evening, I found myself waiting in a rose garden, reflecting that each part of the world seemed to have its own peculiar disadvantages for undercover work. During the past few years, in the practice of my profession, I had sloshed through Arctic bogs full of tangled laurel, fought my way across snow-covered mountains, and sweated over deserts full of spiny cacti. Now I had honeysuckle and roses to contend with. Only the people remained the same, and the job.

Having formulated this piece of deep philosophy, I took stock of my surroundings. It was a formal garden, with hedges, shrubs, and ornamental trees all pruned within inches of their lives. Mrs. Sandeman, I learned, was by way of being the local rose authority with a state-wide reputation. I couldn't help wishing she'd concentrated on dahlias or some other thornless species.

From where I stood concealed, I could see the graveled circle in front of the house. All parking space around it was already filled; the vehicles currently arriving discharged the ladies at the front door and were taken around the circle and back towards the gate by the gentlemen, to be parked beside the long, straight, tree-lined lane leading in from the highway. It was a big, well-kept place with a carefully maintained air of antique southern grandeur. One might have thought it dated from the era of carriages and crinolines. The records indicated, however, that it had been constructed less than five years ago with the antiquity built in.

I saw the white Thunderbird convertible drive up. Teddy Michaelis got out and waited on the steps while Orcutt parked the car. She looked like a dressed-up child, standing there, with long white gloves on, and ridiculously high heels, and a short, shiny blue dress with a bubble of a skirt that looked odd and impractical to me; but I don't claim to understand women's fashions. It was too bad, I thought, that she was a screwball; even at that distance, she was cute.

It would have been nice if the Rostens had managed to arrive while she was standing there alone, so she could do her stuff right off, but you can't have everything. Orcutt came back and escorted her inside, treating her like a precious and fragile work of art. It was another fifteen minutes, and practically dark, before the yellow Cadillac came along.

Mrs. Rosten was wearing something straight, white, and dramatic that left one shoulder bare. She had furs draped over her arm. The white dress showed up well, but her sunburned skin seemed to melt into the dusk, for a rather eerie effect. She paused only briefly on the steps, to shake out the furs and drape them about her; no waiting around in the night air for her. She marched inside, leaving Louis to make it on his own.

I watched him park the car down the lane, return on foot, and vanish inside. I checked my watch and decided it would be at least half an hour before anything happened. At last I backed myself out of my place of concealment, ran the gauntlet of Mrs. Sandeman's thorns, made my way cautiously across the lawn, and got into the rear of the Rosten Cadillac.

I was tempted to sit up until I saw somebody actually approaching from the house, but that would have been sloppy technique. You never know who's going to be wandering around at a party like that, peeking into parked cars for kicks. I checked my watch again and lay down on the floor where I wasn't likely to be noticed—in Petroni's dark suit—unless somebody actually opened the door and pulled the front seat out of the way to make a thorough inspection. That's one advantage of two-door cars, but I don't suppose the advertising boys can do much with it.

I wasn't comfortable, and time passed slowly. It was another half-hour, plus about seven-and-a-half minutes, before I heard my lady coming. She was walking fast, and she had long legs and a business-like stride, but even on the gravel you could tell she was a woman hampered by high heels and a narrow dress. She jerked the car door open, hit the front seat hard, and bounced herself over about ten inches to line up with the wheel. She slammed the door closed. I heard her fumble in her purse for the keys.

"Oh, God *damn!*" she said savagely, as something got in her way.

I received a face-full of mink or sable as she flung her furs in the general direction of the rear seat. Then she had the keys. I waited until she had put the right one into the ignition lock for me; then, under cover of the noise of the starter, I rose up and got a head-hold with my left arm, covering her mouth at the same time, locking my hands together, holding her head hard against me as she writhed and tried to cry out. I used the leverage of both arms to exert knuckle pressure upon a certain nerve center in a certain way. Her body went slack with frightening abruptness.

I couldn't help remembering Jean, and the little sigh she'd given as she crumpled to the floor. I was tempted to feel for a pulse, but there was no time for sentimental horsing around. I got out the little kit we're issued—the one that contains a number of fascinating chemicals, including the death pill for the agent's own use—and slipped the needle, already loaded, into Mrs. Rosten's arm. That would keep her under for about four hours, if she wasn't already dead and if I'd judged the dose correctly.

I dragged her out from behind the wheel, climbed over, started the big car, and drove out of there fast, like an angry woman might—or a man with a limp female body beside him. It took me about half an hour to make my way through town and out the shore road where I'd been that afternoon. The little woods track leading to Mason's Cove wasn't easy to locate in the dark, but I found it, and drove into the clearing where I'd met Rosten earlier, hoping that nobody had decided to use it for a lovers' lane tonight.

The place was empty of vehicles. I checked Mrs. Rosten's pulse and found it strong and steady, which was a relief. I cut the lights and motor, got out and prowled around in the dark, and saw nothing. I sat down to wait. It was a very quiet place. One car went by on the shore road, sounding far away; that was all. There was no wind. There was a mist; I could see stars through the treetops, but they looked vague and distant. Well, I wasn't expecting trouble from that direction, but if anybody on this planet was planning to interfere with the grim work for which I'd been hired twice, it was about time he—or she—showed up.

Nobody came. The moon rose, big and hazy through the trees. A little wind came up and died away. Some small nocturnal animals got used to my presence and went about their nightly affairs. An owl hooted far off, then closer and then far off again. It was a weird sound to hear in the middle of the night. I couldn't help wondering if it had some sinister significance, but after all, I wasn't Daniel Boone surrounded by hostile redskins. I didn't think the people I was after would go in for bird calls, although I still didn't know anything about them. All I knew was Mac's verdict: *They must learn not to monkey with the buzz saw when it is busy cutting wood.*

There was a slight sound from the car, as if the woman I'd left there had stirred in her drugged sleep. I went back and turned on the light to look at her. She'd changed position on the seat; the drug was wearing off. I regarded her for a moment, feeling kind of guilty about the whole thing; but I was committed now. I'd hoped my well-announced murder would get some action out of somebody; but nobody was cooperating. There was nothing to do but carry out the bluff to the end.

I went to work grimly, picking up Mrs. Rosten's purse

and slipping the shoes from her feet. She wasn't wearing stockings; she was tanned enough, I guess, to figure she could get by without them. I carried the stuff halfway across the beach and arranged it neatly on the sand. Then I went back to the Cadillac, started it, and drove forward, out onto the beach, until I felt the wheels begin to sink and slip. I tested reverse, and the rear tires only dug in deeper, indicating that nobody was going to drive the big car out of there, now, without a considerable amount of preliminary work.

I got out, walked around, opened the other door, and got Mrs. Rosten into my arms. I carried her across the beach, out into waist-deep water and threw her in.

14

It was a stupid damn business. By the time I had fished her up and towed her back and arranged her artistically at the water's edge, I felt like a prize damn fool. Soaking wet, with water squelching in my sharp Petroni shoes, I made my way back up the beach disgustedly, and stepped behind the car to watch and wait.

It didn't take long. The cold water had brought her around. I saw her head come up. Her long dark hair, washed free of combs and pins, covered her face like seaweed. She pushed strands of hair from her eyes, sitting up in the shallows, and looked around dazedly, regarding her surroundings and herself with shock and horror. I could hardly blame her. She'd left a gay party and got into her expensive car, something had happened that she couldn't quite remember, and now she was discovering herself in the sodden wreckage of her party finery washed up like driftwood on a dark and lonely shore...

I saw her draw a long breath and take her runaway

emotions under firm control. She got to her feet, took a couple of steps to dry land, and stood there looking around in the moonlight, rubbing her hands on her hips to get the wet sand off them. Now there was something aggressive and challenging, something startlingly primitive in the way she stood there, brown and tall and lean, with her bare feet planted solidly in dry sand, well apart. The wet white cocktail dress could have been a scrap of hide or woven bark. Plastered to her body unheeded, leaving one tanned shoulder bare, it gave her a look of barbaric nakedness. All she needed, I thought, was a stone-tipped spear, and maybe a tame ocelot for a pet. The damn cat didn't need to be very tame, at that. She could handle it.

She stood there, looking and listening warily. I saw her take notice of the Cadillac, stuck in the sand, and I saw her discover her shoes and purse, closer at hand. Presently she moved over and studied them, frowning. She shrugged, and at last gave some attention to her dress, twisting the skirt up hard against her thigh to force the water out of it.

After yanking the wrung-out garment into some kind of order, she squeezed the excess water from her hair and found something in her purse with which to tie the hair back out of the way. She stepped into her shoes, and moved towards the car, but froze as I stepped into sight and came towards her.

"You didn't have to wake up," I said, stopping in front of her.

"You!" she breathed. "What are you doing here? What in God's name do you think you're—what do you want?"

"You didn't have to wake up," I said. "I could have arranged it the other way, too. Call it an object lesson, Mrs. Rosten."

"I'll kill you for this," she said softly. "I will! I'll shoot you down like a dog, Peters—or are you Petroni tonight?"

"Let's say Petroni," I said. "Peters is a harmless jerk."

"The inference being that you're not harmless? You're threatening me?"

I looked at her sadly, and sighed. "Lady, it's not a threat, it's a demonstration. I'm showing you how easy it would be. The only reason you're still alive is because I wanted you that way." I paused deliberately. "You should have come to the phone when I called you this morning, Mrs. Rosten."

"I see," she breathed. "I see. So that's it!"

"I don't call up people just to pass the time of day, not people like you. You could have figured that out, if you'd got off your high horse for a moment. I was trying to do you a favor. You threatened me with cops. You didn't even do it yourself; you had your maid do it. That wasn't smart. That wasn't smart at all."

It was a funny interview. It's hard for a man to be menacing with his pants hanging wet and baggy down his legs, but it's equally hard for a woman to be regal with her dress dripping water into her shoes. We were on even terms, except that she didn't know what I was after, and I did. At least I hoped I did.

I went on, "That little mistake cost you a cocktail outfit and a trip to the beauty parlor, lady. Well, you can afford it. But the next time you get on that arrogant kick, it could cost you something you can't afford to lose, no matter how rich and pretty you are."

Her eyes widened. "My God! That's what it's all about! I hurt his damn little feelings!"

"Yeah," I said. "You hurt my feelings, Mrs. Rosten." I took out the wad of bills I'd collected from her husband and Teddy and slapped it against my hand. "Right here, you hurt my feelings. In the money department."

She lost some of her confidence. "I—I don't understand."

"Have you any idea where I got all this money, five grand?" She looked at me questioningly. "Hell, where are your brains, lady? What do you think we're doing here? This is a down payment. I get the rest when I kill you."

There was a little silence. She was really shocked; this explanation hadn't occurred to her.

"*Kill* me? But *who*—"

"Who hired me?" I laughed. "I'm not likely to tell you that. I've got principles; besides, it would be bad for my reputation if certain people heard I'd given a client's name away. But I'm a businessman, Mrs. Rosten. I said to myself, somebody's willing to pay to have this dame killed, okay. But maybe she'll up the ante, Petroni. Maybe she's willing to pay more *not* to be killed. So I called you, to give you a chance for your life, and you gave me cops. Through the maid, yet! You're damn lucky to be alive, that's all I can say!"

She drew a long breath. "I—all right, what's your proposition?"

I said, "Go home and wring yourself out. I don't like talking to dames who look like they'd been drowned a week. Then get on the phone and call me at the Calvert Hotel, Room 311. I'll be waiting. For a while. Don't make me wait too long, Mrs. Rosten. And I hope I don't have to tell you to keep your trap shut or the deal's off." I looked at her bleakly. "You'll ask me to your home for a sociable drink, in private. And you'll say please."

She said quickly, "If you think for one moment that even to save my life I'd—" She stopped.

I grinned in what I hoped was a sinister fashion. "Did you ever see a floater, Mrs. Rosten?"

"A floater?"

"You were well on the way to being one tonight," I said. "A floater's a stiff that's been fished out of the drink. They generally come up after a while, no matter how they're weighted. They build up gas or something and swell up and break loose and come to the top, what the fishes and crabs have left of them. Then the doc does the autopsy with a gas mask on, and the cops take strips of skin off the fingers and try to restore the prints because nobody's going to recognize the bloated thing on the table except maybe from its jewelry or the few stinking rags wrapped around it." I looked her up and down, as if measuring her for the part. "You call me. Ask me over. Nicely, remember. No maids with any more crummy messages. No maids at all. No servants. No husbands.

And don't think it over too damn long. If you do, lady, you're dead."

I turned and walked away, past the stranded Cadillac. She was no hothouse flower; she'd get it out in time, but it would take some bare-handed digging and several trips into the thorn-and-honeysuckle jungle for brush to put under the rear wheels. By the time she got through, I figured, her appearance and disposition would really be something to witness.

Well, there would be witnesses when she got home, if Teddy and Rosten had followed instructions.

15

I picked up my car in the woods nearby, where I'd hidden it earlier, waiting for Rosten. She was already trying to get the Cadillac loose; I could hear her spinning the wheels as I drove away. Back in my hotel room, I shed my wet clothes in the middle of the rug, and got into the flashy pair of silk pajamas that went with my hoodlum act.

There was no point in sitting by the phone like a teen-aged maiden waiting for a date. If it rang, I'd hear it. I got into bed and fell asleep at once, and dreamed of a dark goddess rising from the sea with a shining spear. I knew the spear was meant for me, and I watched her approach while the great cat stalked majestically by her side, ready to spring if I should move a muscle... The phone rang. I sat up, made a face at my subconscious, and looked at my watch. I'd slept an hour and a half, if you could call it sleeping.

The phone rang again. I picked it up and said, "Yeah?"

"Petroni?" It wasn't at all the voice I'd expected to hear. "Jim?"

"Yeah," I said.

"Jim, this is Teddy. Teddy Michaelis."

"Yeah," I said.

"I—I'm down in the lobby. Can I come up?"

"You can try," I said. "If you make it, the door will be unlocked. Turn the knob and you might even be able to fight your way into the room. I'll be plugging for you all the way."

I hung up, rose, fixed the lock, and heaved my discarded clothes into the bathroom. I combed my hair and put on slippers and a dressing gown that a Chicago tart might have found irresistible if she were drunk and not wearing her contact lenses. Mac had really gone all out to costume me for the part. It shouldn't have bothered me. After all, I'd worn a Nazi uniform a couple of times in the line of duty, and sung the Horst Wessel in guttural German, and said nasty things about Jews. Being a Grade B gangster was a breeze.

I heard the rapping of high heels outside and turned to face the door. Teddy slipped into the room, eased the door closed, and leaned against it, breathless, clutching a small blue satin purse to her bosom. I noticed the purse first. It seemed to contain something considerably bulkier than it had been designed for.

"Well," I said, "what's this all about?" Then I looked at her more sharply. "What the hell happened to you?"

It was a bad night for fashion. The long white gloves were gone, and the shiny blue dress had got a drink spilled down the front. The extravagant bubble skirt was crushed as if she'd been sleeping in it, making love in it, or at least lying down in it very carelessly, perhaps crying. Her small face seemed to bear out the last hypothesis. It had the unbecoming blotched look that follows an emotional crisis accompanied by tears.

"What's the pitch, bitch?" I demanded. "Who broke your doll?"

She looked at me for a moment, and made a sniffing noise. "Here," she said, shoving the purse at me. "Here, take it!"

I glanced at her, took the purse, and opened it cautiously. It was stuffed full of money.

"Go on!" she gasped. "T-take it. It's all there, the rest of your d-dirty five thousand dollars. Take it and go. Go away. Go far, far away. I—I'd tell you to go to hell, but I wouldn't wish you on anybody, not even the d-devil himself!"

She sniffed again, loudly. The phone rang. I picked it up. A deeper voice than the kid's, but still female and familiar, started to speak in my ear.

I said, "I'm busy. Call back in half an hour."

"But—"

"You heard me. Call back."

"Well, really! I must say!"

I hung up on my dark goddess with her well-reallys and her I-must-says. It would do the haughty Mrs. Rosten good, from Lash Petroni's viewpoint, and maybe even from Matt Helm's, to stew a little longer. The fact that she'd called at all meant that I'd won something, although

I still wasn't quite sure what. I turned back to the kid, took a clean handkerchief from my pocket and placed it in her hand.

"Blow your nose and tell Papa Petroni all about it."

She looked at my handkerchief and threw it on the floor and ran the back of her hand and forearm back and forth under her nose, defiantly. I guess the unladylike gesture was supposed to shock me.

"All right," I said. "If you spurn my hanky, have a drink instead—and don't tell me you won't touch my lousy liquor. That's enough temperament for tonight. I read your message loud and clear: you don't like me any more."

"I hate you! I don't know how I could have—"

"Skip it," I said. I pocketed the money and gave her little purse back. "Now go into the bathroom and wash your face. Other cosmetic and sartorial improvements may occur to you, once you look in the mirror. One might even say the field is wide open."

"I won't—"

"Go on," I said, swinging her around and giving her a slap behind. She started indignantly.

"Don't touch me!"

"Don't worry, I'm not contagious."

She glared at me over her shoulder. "Oh, yes, you are! If it hadn't been for you, I'd never have dreamed of—"

The phone rang again. It was my busy night. If it kept up like this, I'd have to hire a secretary. I closed the bathroom door on Teddy's rumpled, rebellious little figure, and crossed the room. This time it was the male half of the Rosten duo on the line. It sounded as if he were calling from a bar or all-night restaurant; there was jukebox music in the background.

"Petroni, I have to talk to you—"

"In the morning," I said.

"But I must know what went wrong—"

"In the morning," I said. "I'll get in touch."

I hung up on Louis and made the drinks, trying not to feel too pleased with myself. I might not know any more than I had before, but at least I had them all buzzing like angry bees. The kid came out of the bathroom looking subdued and, except for her stained dress, almost respectable. I put a glass into her hand.

"Who was on the phone?" she asked.

"None of your damn business," I said. "Don't get nosy."

She flushed. "You don't have to be rude!"

I said, "Easy, Teddy. I never told you the devil didn't deserve you. I figure I've still got some change coming, as far as rudeness is concerned."

She looked up at me and drew a long, ragged breath. Her eyes were big and shiny in her tiny face. "I—I don't understand you, Jim. I don't understand myself. I know you're a dreadful person, and I tell myself I hate and despise you, and then I come here and—and you're almost human in your funny, overbearing way, and I—oh, I don't know what I'm trying to say!" She gulped at her drink, and looked up again. "What happened? What went wrong with your plans?"

"What makes you think something went wrong?"

"Well, Mrs. Rosten—she escaped, didn't she? She came home a mess, but alive and hopping mad." Before I could offer an excuse or explanation, Teddy shook her head quickly. "Never mind. I don't want to know anything about it. I don't care, just so she's alive. Why—why, I might be a murderess now!" She glanced at me. "It's all right, isn't it? You have your money, all of it. I don't mind. I must have been insane! I deserve—I don't mind about the money. But you will go away, won't you—and forget I ever asked you to—It was horrible," she breathed. "Simply horrible!"

"What was horrible?"

"All that waiting at the house, making conversation, trying to act natural, not knowing how we'd hear. I thought I'd throw up when the telephone rang, honest! And then hearing her car come up the drive like a maniac was at the wheel, or somebody who'd been—terribly hurt and was trying to get home before—before she—passed out or died." The childish blue eyes looked up at me, remembering. "And the car screeched to a halt outside, and we heard her get out and stumble up the steps—and I remembered what you'd said about—about smashed faces and ripped out fingernails. I thought I'd die, watching that door, waiting to see what—I wouldn't go through another minute like that for a million dollars!"

I said, "You hate Mrs. Rosten. She's responsible for your daddy's death. Remember?"

Teddy didn't seem to hear. "And then she was standing

there like that, like a—a tattered ghost, like something that had clawed its way out of a damp grave, and I knew if she saw my face she'd know, and I managed to spill my drink—" Her voice trailed off.

"Quick thinking," I said. "Did it work?"

"I think so. I don't think she suspects. I'm going back to New York in the morning," Teddy said breathlessly. "I should never have come! I've made a perfect little fool of myself! Why, I really haven't any proof at all, have I? I guess I was just, well, dramatizing. I just don't know what I was thinking of!"

I looked down at her for a little while without speaking. It was the first clear profit of the evening's work: I could cross one name off the list. She wasn't acting. She honestly believed she'd just missed becoming a blood-stained criminal; which meant she believed in her ruthless accomplice, the criminal Lash Petroni. She had no suspicion she was talking to a phony. Whoever had listened to those tapes recorded in Jean's room, it wasn't she.

I felt kind of sorry for the little girl, standing there with her prettiness tarnished and her self-confidence destroyed. A night's sleep and a change of clothes would fix her up in one respect, but it would take some time before she got over the shock of discovering that she wasn't nearly as wicked as she'd thought. I was tempted to let it go at that; but this was no time for sentimentality. I couldn't afford to let her off the hook as long as there was a possibility of her exerting useful pressure on one of the others.

I took the purse from her hands, got the money from my dressing gown pocket, and stuffed it back the way it had been. I put the purse into her hands.

She said quickly, "But I *want* you to have it."

"I'll have it," I said. "When I've earned it."

She stared at me, wide-eyed. "But you can't—I mean, you don't have to—I mean, I don't want—"

"Who the hell," I said, "cares what you want, now? You started the ball rolling, how are you going to call it back? Go to New York, go anywhere you please. You'll know when the payoff is due. You'll read about it in the papers. You have the dough ready. Okay?"

"No!" she gasped. "No, it's not okay. You must be crazy!"

"You had your chance to pull out this afternoon," I said. "Don't talk crazy to me, doll. At least I don't change my mind sixteen times a minute. I've got this thing going now, I'm looking forward to doing a job on that snooty dame, and you're not chickening out on Lash Petroni, understand? What the hell do you think this is, anyway? You don't turn a guy like me on and off like a lavatory spigot!" I had her by the arm, leading her towards the door. "Now get out of here—"

As I reached for the knob, it was turned from outside; I stepped back, shoving Teddy aside. The door opened, showing young Orcutt standing on the threshold. He looked at me and he looked at the kid.

"I thought," he said quietly to her, "you might be just about ready to leave, Teddy."

She hesitated, sniffed, and ran to him. "Oh, Billy!"

I asked, "Do you spend your life trailing her around, Billy?"

He said, "It is my ambition to do so, sir." He caught sight of himself in the dresser mirror, straightened his tie, and put his arm around the girl. "I'm working on it, you might say." For all of being a plump boy, he had a kind of impressive dignity.

"There's some risk involved in a plan like that."

"You made that quite plain the last time we met, sir. I'm afraid my performance wasn't very noteworthy." He paused, and went on, "Just the same, I will tell you again what I told you then. Leave her alone, Mr. Petroni. I don't know what's between you and I don't care. Just stay clear away from her, hear? The next time—"

"What about next time, punk?" I asked sneeringly.

"The next time," he said gently, "you'll have to kill me. Come on, Teddy. My car's downstairs. I'll take you back to the motel."

I watched them go out, frowning. There might be less to little Teddy Michaelis, as far as the case was concerned, than had appeared at first, but young Orcutt, with his habit of popping up at odd moments, was becoming more and more interesting.

The phone started ringing behind me. I closed the door and looked at my watch. Mrs. Rosten was calling back right on time; it had been exactly half an hour since her previous call. I shivered, for some reason, as I went to talk to her.

16

It was a large place on the water, some distance out of town. By the time I reached it, the moon was getting low and a mist was rising. My headlights sent long white fingers searching the lawns and trees ahead of me as I followed the winding drive around to the rear of the house, as instructed. There wasn't a breath of air moving. The small sound as the house door opened seemed as loud as a gunshot.

"This way," Mrs. Rosten called softly. I got out of the car and joined her. She said, "I apologize for the back door, but I thought you'd rather not attract any more attention than necessary."

I said, "It couldn't just be that you're ashamed of your guest, lady."

She was wearing something long and pale that whispered when she swung to face me. I couldn't see her face clearly, but her voice was sharp, "Can't you forget that twisted pride for one minute, Petroni? I said please over the phone, didn't I?"

She turned away, leaving me to follow her ghostlike figure through a dark kitchen and a succession of dark rooms into a small, softly lighted, booklined study in which a fire was burning. I noted a gun rack over the fireplace. A leather sofa faced the fireplace. It looked quite comfortable and inviting. On the low table before the sofa was a silver tray holding an array of bottles, two glasses, a silver ice bucket, and so help me, a real honest-to-God soda-water siphon. I hadn't seen one of those in years.

She had stopped to close the door behind me. I turned to face her. We stood like that for a moment. I pursed my lips and whistled softly.

"Not bad. That must be just about the quickest recovery in history."

She'd got her hair up again, drawn back smoothly from her face. It had a dark, velvety luster she must have worked hard to attain in such a short time. I don't know the technical distinction between a negligee and a peignoir, but she was wearing one of those elaborate boudoir creations, creamy white against her brown skin, high-necked and long-sleeved, lace to the waist and layers upon layers of nylon below, reaching the floor all around her.

In this day of trick pajamas and Peter Pan nighties, it's a real treat to see an attractive woman dressed for seduction in a garment with some grace and dignity to it. It raises the whole business of sex to a higher plane, in my opinion. I assumed that seduction was what she had in mind, dressing like that—or at least that it was the idea she wished to plant in Lash Petroni's crude mind, for reasons yet to be determined. In a way it was a relief. I hadn't been sure she wouldn't greet me with a shotgun, or the police.

"You have the tact of an ox, Petroni," she said. "Never remind a woman of looking like hell, particularly when it was your fault. Come to that, you look a little better yourself."

That was a lie. I'd seen myself in the mirror as I left the hotel room in my other Petroni suit. The man who'd looked back at me from the glass had been a real cool cat. I wouldn't have trusted him in the same house with Whistler's grandmother.

"It's a wet damn bay," I said.

"Let's drink to that," she said, smiling. "It's something we can agree on, anyway. What will you have?"

I watched her sweep past and bend over the silver tray. There wasn't any peekaboo stuff; there were no provocative displays of skin or limbs such as often go with the negligee bit. She was a great lady entertaining at home, but I couldn't help the distracting thought—as Lash Petroni, of course—that dignified though she might look in the regal gown, she probably had on very little underneath it.

I cleared my throat and said, "Bourbon and water, lady. Hell, make it soda. I haven't seen one of those fizz-water machines in action since I was a kid."

"Is that so?"

She tried to sound interested, but her smile was mechanical. The polite mask slipped for just a moment. She didn't give a damn what Petroni had or had not seen as a kid, and the idea of pretending to be fascinated by the horrible creature's revolting childhood turned her stomach. But she caught herself, and brought my drink to me, and smiled again, doing a better job this time.

"Sit down, please," she said, and laughed softly. "There! I said it again. Please." She moved towards the couch. "Where did you grow up, Petroni—Jim? That's your name, isn't it? Jim?"

"That's it," I said. "Jim."

"You may call me Robin."

"Okay, Robin."

She sank down on the couch, and patted the space beside her. "*Please* sit down. You make me nervous standing over me like that. You must be just about the tallest man I know. Did you play basketball as a boy, Jim?"

It was time to exert a bit of pressure. She couldn't be allowed to think Petroni was a complete fool. I looked down at her deliberately, and gave her a slow, mean grin.

"Cut it out, lady. All you have to be is polite. If there's any seducing to be done, I'll do it."

Sitting there, she looked up quickly. I saw hatred flame in her dark eyes, but only for an instant. Then she was laughing.

"All right," she said, "all right, Jim. I deserved that. I underestimated you. I was only testing my weapons, if you know what I mean."

"I know what you mean." I sat down beside her. "Let's not worry about my childhood. You don't give a damn about my lousy childhood. Have you got anything on under all that glamor?" I touched the filmy stuff of her skirt, draped across the leather sofa between us.

It caught her by surprise. "Why—why, just a nightgown," she said.

"I bet it's real pretty," I said. "Maybe we'll get to it later. Right now I figure we've got other business than my childhood and your lingerie, but don't give up hope."

That brought her to her feet. Two quick steps took her to the fireplace. She reached up, and swung to face me with a double-barreled shotgun in her hands. The business-like weapon, though very handsome for a gun, went oddly with the feminine fragility of her appearance.

"You despicable creature!" she said. "You revolting animal! Just because you force me to be civil to you doesn't mean—" She stopped.

I yawned deliberately, and gave her that mean Petroni grin again. "So," I said, "now we know. Wet or dry, you're still a snooty bitch, and I'm still a revolting animal, and any resemblance to nice people having a cozy drink before making beautiful music is strictly, like they say in the movies, coincidental." I swung my feet up on the couch, and leaned back with a sigh of contentment. "Ah, that's better. It's been a long, busy day. Put the blaster away, honey. I figured you had one loaded and ready somewhere. It was either that or cops; you'd want some protection from a despicable creature like me."

"Get your damn feet off my furniture!"

I yawned again. "Cut it out, sweetheart. You've proved you're not a pushover. I've proved I'm not a pushover. Let's stop making faces at each other, huh?"

I tasted my drink without looking at her or the gun, which wasn't as easy as it sounds. At that range, a twelve-gauge would take my head off if she got careless with the trigger. I was relieved when she laughed shortly and put back the weapon. Nylon whispered as she moved away across the room. I turned my head at last and saw her standing at the window, looking out. After a while, I set my drink aside and went to stand behind her.

The big study window looked down on a dark harbor with a T-shaped dock. There were lights on the dock. Some sailboats were anchored or moored farther out; they seemed to be floating in mist. A power cruiser with a broad, square stern displaying twin exhausts and the name *Osprey* lay along the stem of the T; and a big white schooner was tied across the far end. Apparently the *Freya* had been brought out of hiding after the story in the paper. A lighted porthole indicated that somebody was on board. Well out beyond the harbor, an arching chain of lights hung over the mist, reaching off across the Bay.

"I hate that damn Bay Bridge," Robin Rosten said abruptly. "We used to have a ferry, you know. It was picturesque and—well nice. They wrecked my farm, some of the best land in the state, to build that bridge right after the war. You didn't know I was a farmer, did you, Jim?"

"No," I said. "I didn't know."

"I was, though. Louis couldn't understand that; he thinks when you have money all you ought to do is sit back and spend it. He couldn't understand why I wanted to go around in boots, smelling like a barn. I had a beautiful dairy farm north of here; and they ran their approach highway right through the middle of it. Four lanes of concrete and a fence. They wouldn't even let us cross it. We had to go halfway to town to use the north pasture, which wasn't really practical. You don't know why I'm telling you this, do you?"

"No," I said. I put my hands on her shoulders. "But you go right ahead and tell me. I'm listening."

"Easy," she murmured without turning her head. "Take it very easy, Jim. I don't like to be mauled."

"Nobody's mauling you," I said. "I wouldn't maul you."

She laughed. "You have a very short memory."

"That's different," I said.

"You're a horrible man."

"Sure."

"I still haven't got all the sand out of my hair. How did you know I wouldn't call the police?"

"Some chances you've got to take. I thought you'd rather deal, one way or another. It was a gamble."

"What would you have done if I had called them?"

"I had a story to tell."

"I know. I saw the way you left my shoes and purse on the beach."

"There was this crazy society dame, see, who got drunk and tried to drown herself. Petroni just happened along in time to fish her out."

"It's a ridiculous story."

"Maybe. I had answers to most of the questions, not good, but good enough. I've got people who'll hire lawyers for me, as good as yours. It would have been your word against mine. And afterwards you'd have got another phone call. And if you'd sent the maid with a snotty message this time, well, the rich Mrs. Rosten might just kind of managed to bump herself off on the second try. I was laying the ground work, you might say."

"You're a dreadful person," she said. "Leave my zipper alone, darling. I don't like to be picked at." She reached back and caught my hands and brought them forward, and leaned back against me, inside the circle of my arms, holding my hands to her breasts. "There's a cheap thrill for you, you despicable creature," she said without turning her head.

There wasn't anything under my hands but Robin Rosten and some lace. It was, let's say, a disturbing sensation, even for a man as devoted to his country's interests, as dedicated to his mission, as that grim, implacable undercover operative, Matthew Helm.

I cleared my throat and said, "Which brings up the question, why does the aristocratic Mrs. Rosten, instead of simply having him arrested, invite a nasty hoodlum into the house to fondle her tits."

She stiffened against me. "Don't be coarse." Then

she laughed and relaxed. "I like you, Petroni. You've got a refreshing directness. And you don't pretend to be something you aren't."

Here was another woman telling me I wasn't pretending, sincerely or otherwise. I remembered something else Teddy Michaelis had said. I'd have to put the kid straight. She'd done the older woman an injustice. They weren't spectacularly large, but they'd certainly be missed.

"Everybody likes Petroni," I said. "You haven't answered my question."

"You know the answer."

"You want to know who hired me," I said. "And you didn't think the police would get it out of me. Smart girl. But I told you at the cove, I've got principles."

"Still?" she murmured, warm in my arms.

"Cut it out," I said. "You're making the mistake dames always make. They all think their bodies have got something to do with business."

She was silent for a moment; then her soft laughter came again. "Rebuked, by God! Petroni, you're wonderful! It was Louis, wasn't it?" I didn't say anything, and she went on, "Oh, don't bother to deny it. He was pretty obvious about picking a quarrel with me so I'd drive off alone. And I saw his face when I came home. He'd never expected to see me alive again; he was absolutely petrified. He's off getting drunk right now, recovering from the shock. He'd have betrayed himself right there if that odd little girl, Michaelis' idiot child, hadn't managed to spill whisky all over herself, gawking. That gave him time to recover, helping to mop her off. You know Louis. If the world was coming to an end, he still wouldn't pass up the chance to pat a pretty girl with a paper towel."

"You know Louis," I said. "I didn't say I knew Louis."

She patted my hands lightly, and lifted them away, disengaging herself. "I think that's enough erotic stimulation for the moment. Where's my drink?"

"Where you left it," I said. "Erotic stimulation. That's fancy for kicks? I'll have to remember it."

"I didn't think Louis would have the nerve to kill me," she said, moving towards the coffee table. "Or even hire someone to have it done. Of course, he's been acting strangely of late, ever since Norman disappeared. I wonder."

She gave me my glass as I came up. I took it and said, "Thanks. I still haven't said anything."

She smiled, raising her own glass to me. "Keep your damn principles. I know it was Louis. The only question is why."

"I'm not saying one way or another. But if he did want you killed, I could think of a reason."

"Money?" She shook her head. "Louis wouldn't kill for money. Oh, I don't mean he doesn't like it; but he's even more cowardly than he's greedy. He's a rat; he'll only bite if he's cornered and scared, really scared."

"That's a hell of a way to talk about your own husband."

She ignored the comment. "Louis has been scared ever since we found Norman's boat empty; scared I'd noticed something, I guess. Only it goes back farther. I think dear

Louis has got himself involved in something big and dangerous, so big and dangerous he has to kill his way out. Did he ever mention Mendenhall to you?"

"Mendenhall?" I said. "What's that? And who's Norman?"

"Mendenhall used to be the family estate; it's part of a restricted Marine training area now. Norman was—is a friend of mine. He vanished mysteriously some weeks ago. Louis must have told you."

"Don't be clever. Why should he tell me and when? For the record, I've only seen your damn husband a couple of times in my life, and talked to him, never. What about this Mendenhall place?"

"The government took it away from me," she said. "We talk big about how bad they have it over there, with the dirty communists and their tyranny; and all the time we've got our own little bureaucratic tyrants right here, with their confiscatory income taxes and ruthless condemnation proceedings. Well, never mind all that. The funny thing is, Louis was almost as upset as I was when it happened, although he doesn't give a damn about the family. He's been fascinated by Mendenhall for years, for some reason, particularly the island—"

"The island?" I couldn't help asking the question. "What island?"

She didn't seem to notice that I'd stepped out of character, if I had. "Well, it wasn't originally an island," she said. "Originally, when the land was first settled, it was a peninsula, a long, wooded point of land; and the first house was built out there among the pines, facing the little bay. Then the land gradually washed away, and even the big house—a hurricane took that in the eighteen-seventies—and the family rebuilt on the mainland. There's nothing out there now but a chain of little islets and one real island about a mile by a half with a stand of pines and a few old ruins, all cut off from the mainland by a mile of shallows and an eight-foot channel washed out by the tide."

I said, "Geography is interesting, honey—history, too—but I like erotic stimulation better."

I hoped my voice was level and casual; and I hoped my words wouldn't discourage her from telling me more, but I didn't really think they would. She wanted to tell me all this—she wanted to tell Lash Petroni all this. The question was, why?

She said, "I used to play there as a girl. We'd sail down and have picnics. I took Louis once, just to show him, before we were married; but he's not the picnic type. It wasn't until a few years ago that he began to act interested. He had us anchor in the little bay a few times, cruising in the *Freya*, while he rowed ashore and explored. That was before the government took it. I have a feeling that whatever he's got himself into, it's got something to do with Mendenhall Island."

I said, "But if the Marine Corps has got it now, and it's restricted as you say—"

She laughed. "You're not a sailor, are you? They don't build many fences in the water, Jim. On a dark night, in a sailing vessel like the *Freya* down there, I could ghost right into Mendenhall Bay without a sentry noticing a thing. I don't think they use their radars except when they're actually firing. The question is, just what is Louis up to? There was that strange business about Norman; all kinds of government people were around asking questions."

It was time for me to ask some more questions about the mysterious Norman, or maybe it wasn't. I didn't like that casual reference to government people.

I said, "Look, honey, this is fascinating as hell, but what's it got to do with me?"

She said, "It depends on Louis. I don't mind so much his trying to have me killed, although it does seem to indicate he's cracking up, doesn't it? And if he slipped out in a boat and hit Norman over the head with an oar that afternoon because he was jealous, well, I gave him lots of provocation. It would be kind of nice to think he still cared that much." She shook her head abruptly. "I don't believe it for a moment. I think he's mixed up in something big and nasty. And if he thinks he's going to involve the family and me in some dirty scandal—He'll get caught, of course. He hasn't got the brains not to. Unless—"

"Unless what?"

She drained her glass and set it down on the table. It was low enough, and she was tall enough, so that she had to bend down a bit to make it.

"I'll pay well, of course," she said in a matter-of-fact tone.

"Sure," I said. "For what, and how well?"

She smiled at me, and made a slight gesture towards the drink in my hand. I finished it off, and put the glass down beside hers.

"I'd pay very well indeed, Jim Petroni," she said, holding out her hands.

"I like cash," I said.

She laughed, unoffended. "You're a cold, stubborn man. There'll be cash, too."

Then she was in my arms, or vice versa. I can't lay claim to having originated the idea; but I saw no reason to fight it for that reason. Jimmy the Lash wouldn't be likely to put up a violent defense for his virtue. As for that sterling government employee, Matt Helm, I found it difficult to remember exactly who I was, of all the people I'd pretended to be, feeling the warmth of her lips and of her long, taut body, unconfined beneath the lace and nylon of the dignified gown. Some men prefer naked women, but I guess I like my presents gift wrapped, to start with, at least.

"You'll do it, won't you?" she breathed at last. "You'll get rid of him for me?" She laughed, her breath warm on my ear. "I'm rather bored with Louis, anyway, and divorces are so messy and expensive."

I found myself thinking, vaguely, that I'd never come across such a murderous bunch of citizens in my long and bloody career; but to be perfectly honest, I wasn't paying all the attention I might have. Only so much can be accomplished standing up; and I had a certain leather sofa rather strongly in mind.

"Sure, baby," I said thickly. "Anybody. Just name him and he's dead."

That was Lash Petroni speaking, but his voice seemed to come from far away. I drew a long breath and straightened up and looked into Robin Rosten's face. It wouldn't focus clearly; it seemed to waver before me; but I could see that she was smiling oddly. I glanced quickly toward the glasses on the coffee table.

"You bitch," Petroni said, a long ways off.

She laughed, watching me with speculative interest. I had a choice to make; and I reached out and took her by the throat before she could step back. I saw her eyes go shocked and wide.

"Too bad, lady," Petroni said. "Too bad. You shouldn't have tried—"

I made the voice trail off incoherently. The apprehension went out of her eyes as my fingers relaxed. I went to my knees and pitched forward, grasping at her skirt. After a little, I felt her bend over me and free the filmy nylon, tougher and more elastic than it looked.

"Good night," she murmured. "Good night, Matthew Helm—or should I call you Eric?"

As I closed my eyes, I knew I'd found what I'd been looking for: the muffled voice on the telephone, Jean's contact, the person who'd known all along I wasn't a gangster named Petroni...

17

I awoke on a boat. I knew this much about my surroundings before I opened my eyes. There were small, distant wave noises, and there was a certain amount of nautical creaking and groaning—the really big ships don't talk much in ordinary weather, but the smaller ones do, and once you've heard the sound, even if it was a long time ago, you don't forget it. I could hear footsteps on the deck over my head. There was some motion: the limited, rather jerky motion of a vessel lying at a dock and bumping up against it once in a while.

1 knew all this, and I knew there was someone in the room, or cabin, with me. He wasn't noisy, but he breathed and, now and then, shifted position slightly. I opened my eyes and looked at him where he stood leaning against the door because the cabin offered no facilities for sitting except the bunk on which I lay.

He was one of the biggest men I'd ever seen, very black, with a bony shaved head adorned with a curving white scar that looked as if someone had tried to split his skull with a meat cleaver but had failed simply because the tool wasn't up to the job. It would take an ax. He had broad nostrils and a broad, thick-lipped mouth. I suppose you'd call him ugly. He certainly wasn't pretty, but there was a kind of magnificence about him, even in faded denim shirt and pants, that reminded me, somehow, of his mistress—who was also pretty magnificent, I recalled ruefully, if in a different way.

"Hi, Nick," I said.

He leaned there lazily, unmoving. "You know me, man?"

"Nicodemus Jackson," I said, repeating information I'd got from Washington over the phone. "Six-five, two hundred and sixty pounds."

"Two hundred and sixty-five," he said. "I put on a little weight, loafing around up the creek there with nothing to do but polish the brass. I'll go tell Miz Rosten you're awake. She figured you'd be coming around about now." He straightened up, towering above me in the little cabin, and grinned, showing large white teeth. "She's a welded steel schooner, man. Built in Germany before World War II, but still sound as the day she was launched. The hull's steel. The bulkheads are steel. Even this here door—" he gave it a blow that made it ring dully, "is steel, and it's got a powerful strong bolt. The porthole's dogged down tight; you couldn't budge it without a two-foot wrench. You catch my drift? I'd sure hate to see you waste your time and scratch up my paintwork."

"I catch your drift," I said. "What's a bulkhead? Oh, you mean the partitions?" I regarded him for a moment. "You know I'm a government man, Nick? You could get in trouble, keeping me locked up in here."

I had to say it, if only to give him a break if he didn't know, but I didn't expect it to impress him greatly. It didn't. He merely grinned again.

"I don't know nothing," he said. "Miz Rosten, she does the knowing. I just does the doing, if you catch my drift. Miz Rosten takes care of the trouble, if it comes."

Well, that took care of my responsibility towards Big Nick, and I could clobber him with good conscience if I ever had the chance, the strength and a heavy instrument, blunt or edged. With a man that size, it doesn't pay to be particular.

"That program could keep you both pretty busy," I said.

He grinned more broadly. "Man, you don't look like much trouble to me, a skinny gentleman like you." He gestured towards a narrow door. "The head's in there."

"What's a head?" I asked. "Oh, you mean the plumbing?"

"That's right, the plumbing," he said. "Open the seacocks before you pump. I'll go tell Miz Rosten."

He went out silently. I noticed that his feet were bare. The door closed and I heard the bolt go home. It sounded powerful strong, just as he'd said. I was left alone in my quarters, if that's the proper seagoing term for accommodations. It had been a long time since I'd had to remember port from starboard, and I had no intention of revealing the little nautical information I retained. A show of ignorance can be a useful weapon.

Aside from a trick belt buckle—standard equipment—designed primarily for cutting the hands free in an emergency, it was the only weapon I had, unless you included the do-it-yourself suicide kit from my discarded drug supply. Since there was no rope on my wrists, and nothing else around to cut, the buckle wasn't much use at the moment, although it might come in handy later. As for the death pill, concealed never mind where, it might come in handy, too, but I might be forgiven for hoping it wouldn't.

I sat up and looked around. My bunk could be called a tight double or a roomy single. It was equipped with a hinged board at the side which could be raised and locked in place to keep the occupants from being tossed out in rough weather. The cabin was exactly as long as the bunk. It was as wide as the bunk plus a built-in three-drawer dresser. This, at the foot end, took up some of the floor space, leaving only an area of about two feet by four for standing, opening the doors, and pulling on your pants in the morning. Everything was painted white except the woodwork, which was rich mahogany, beautifully varnished, and the floor, which was smooth, unfinished teakwood.

I already had my pants on, as well as the rest of my number two Petroni outfit, somewhat the worse for being slept in. I tried using the handsome teak floor for standing purposes, therefore, and it worked. Whatever my dark sea-goddess had given me last night, it had practically worn off. I felt pretty good, physically speaking.

Mentally speaking, of course, I felt pretty foolish. I mean, as a man, I couldn't very well help thinking of the silent laughs Robin Rosten must have had, last night, playing up to my tough gangster act in her best boudoir regalia, knowing all the time that I was a phony and that she was going to slip me a mickey at the first convenient opportunity. Well, it's always nice to know you've brought a bit of gaiety into somebody's life; and I'd been at this work too long to be sensitive about making myself ridiculous. The sensitive agents, full of pride and dignity, die very young.

I grimaced at my face in the dressing mirror. On the whole, I was doing all right, in my clumsy and blundering way. After all, my job had been to take Jean's place, one way or another. Well, I'd done it, hadn't I? I'd spotted her contact; I was on my way. The train was back on the tracks after temporary derailment. After much maneuvering, we finally had an agent in the hands of the enemy.

Of course, according to plan, Jean would have come aboard with her arm in a cast, containing certain interesting and useful objects embedded in the plaster of Paris. She'd have come aboard as a deserter from our side, presumably trusted to some extent by the other. She might even have got a cabin with a wooden door and a less powerfully strong bolt. I had no trust and very few tools to work with; I was a prisoner instead of a potential ally. Still, I should have been pleased with my progress. It was no time to be thinking of a woman with long, dark hair.

I looked at my face in the mirror above the dresser and didn't like it much. It was, I decided, the face of a ruthless man who'd carry out orders ruthlessly. At least it had better be if I was going to get out of this alive. I went into the bathroom, or head, which was the size of a broom closet. The tiny lavatory drained into the toilet bowl, which in turn could be emptied by means of a couple of valves and a long lever with a shiny brass handle.

There were instructions in German on a shiny brass plate, and in English on a printed card addressed TO OUR LANDLUBBER GUESTS, and enclosed, under glass, in a neat frame above the apparatus. I remembered wrestling with similar pumping equipment on a converted yacht in a storm in the North Sea a good many years ago, at a time when the North Sea wasn't exactly a healthy place to be in any weather. I was interested to see that everything still worked the same, if it worked. The other gadget hadn't.

I performed the usual early-morning operations, cleaning up as well as I could without a razor. I started to follow the printed instructions and stopped, remembering that ignorance was a weapon and a watchword. I went out, leaving the mess sloshing around in the toilet bowl with the schooner's motion.

Presently there was a knock on the door, and Big Nick's voice said, "Lie down on the bed, man."

I lay down on the bed. "All clear," I said.

He opened the door and looked in cautiously. Seeing me flat on my back—a position from which it would be hard to jump him—he opened the door fully and reached back into the hall or passageway outside, and produced a suitcase that I recognized as my own, or Lash Petroni's.

"How'd you get that?" I asked.

He showed me his grin. I was losing faith in that grin. I didn't think Nick was really a nice friendly man. I was remembering an agent named Ames, who'd been found dead on a lonely beach with a broken neck. Robin Rosten didn't quite have the hands for that job, but Nick did.

"Man," he said, "when Miz Rosten sends a Cadillac with a uniformed chauffeur to check out a guest that's going cruising with her, nobody asks no questions."

I said, "I bet you look real sharp in a chauffeur's cap, Nick."

He gave me a quick suspicious glance, and said coldly, "Miz Rosten say for you to shave and put on something that don't make you look like a tinhorn gambler—something shipshape, like. And a pair of rubber-soled shoes. She wants you on deck as soon as we're under way."

I said, "My compliments to Mrs. Rosten, and will you forward my apologies for forgetting to bring my yachting cap?"

"Never mind all the caps," he said, unsmiling. "Just remember the shoes, man. She don't allow no leather shoes on her nice teak deck."

"Sure," I said. "I guess I've got a pair of gumshoes

somewhere. Before you go, brief me on how to flush that damn john. I couldn't make it work."

He glanced into the bathroom and looked at me grimly. Obviously landlubbers were a cross he had to bear, but he didn't have to like it.

"I told you, before you pump, you've got to open the cocks, both of them. One lets the waste out; the other lets seawater in to flush it clean." He looked at my uncomprehending face. "Seacocks," he said wearily. "Like valves, man."

"Oh, valves," I said. "I dig you now, man. I didn't know what the hell you were talking about. Cocks, for God's sake. But why not just leave them open?"

"If she heels over hard in a breeze, she might take some water aboard."

"You mean the damn boat could sink just because somebody went to the can? That doesn't seem like very good planning."

He showed me his big teeth. "Don't you go getting ideas. You ain't going to scuttle her just by leaving those seacocks open. It just kind of splashes around and gets things wet if there's a sea running. So when you're through, you close them, hear, after you've pumped out all the water. There's bad weather down the coast and we might get a little blow—"

A distant voice that I recognized, Robin's voice, called from somewhere above us. "Nick, come here!"

"Coming, ma'am." He moved quickly to the door, and looked back. "Remember the shoes," he said. "She's mighty particular about that deck, Miz Rosten is."

After he had left, bolting the door behind him, I moved to look out the porthole over the bunk. There was gray daylight outside; the sky was overcast. I was looking straight at the high, flaring bow of the power cruiser called *Osprey*, which was rolling quite heavily even in the sheltered harbor. I wondered where the waves were coming from. There didn't seem to be that much wind blowing.

A man ran shoreward along the dock. He was wearing tennis shoes, white ducks, and a yachting cap. I recognized Louis Rosten. Apparently he'd come home, regardless of his fears. Reaching land, he vanished from sight behind the bulk of the powerboat. A moment later a small sports car that I recognized came into view with Rosten at the wheel. It drove up the hill and out of sight past the big house.

While I was puzzling over this, I heard footsteps in the passageway outside. The door opened. I turned to see Robin Rosten standing there with Nick behind her. In front of her was Teddy Michaelis with her arm twisted up between her shoulder blades and tears of pain running down her small face. Robin gave her a shove that sent her across the cabin.

"There's company for you, my actor friend," Robin said to me. "You can have a lot of fun explaining to her that you're an agent named Helm working for the U.S. Government. She seems to be under the impression that you're a killer named Petroni whom she's hired for some nefarious purpose she now regrets. She came here to warn me against you. I think it's really very sweet of her." The taller woman turned to Nick. "Lock them up. We'll shove off as soon as Louis comes back from hiding the little fool's car."

18

When I was brought on deck a couple of hours later, the shoreline from which we'd departed was a low, misty mass off to the right, the way we were heading—to starboard, if you want to be technical about it. I knew it was our shoreline because I'd been keeping track of it through the cabin porthole when Nick came to get me. There was another vague land mass off to the left, presumably the opposite shore of Chesapeake Bay, although it could have been an island.

There seemed to be a moderate breeze from behind us, but strangely enough, the waves were coming from ahead, moving up the Bay to meet us in long, oily swells that made the schooner pitch and roll uneasily as she plowed southward under power.

When I emerged from the hatch or companionway or whatever sailors call the opening in the deckhouse that leads up and out from the main cabin, Louis Rosten was doing something seamanlike at the mainmast. He didn't look at me. Big Nick guided me towards Robin, at the wheel. This was located at the aftermost end of the cockpit, a sunken Roman bathtub sort of depression in the wide deck, with seats all around. Under the seats were slat-front lockers labeled LIFE PRESERVERS. Well, it was nice to know where to look in time of need.

I'm neither a seaman nor a weatherman, but those big rollers coming in against the wind didn't make me very happy. I couldn't help remembering that, according to the newspaper, a tropical disturbance was moving up the coast, and that Nick had said we might run into a bit of weather. The *Freya* looked very big to be handled efficiently, in a serious blow, by the few people visible on deck, one a prisoner.

"Here he is, ma'am," Nick said.

Robin looked up from the compass, and took in my tight, sporty Petroni slacks and flashy zipper jacket. "Well, that's a slight improvement, but you still look like a racetrack tout," she murmured. There was a small silence, while we both remembered, I guess, various intimacies that had passed between us before I lost interest in my surroundings the night before. Anyway, I did. She patted the schooner's steering wheel. "Take the helm. That'll keep your hands busy," she said, and laughed. "Take the helm, Helm."

I stepped forward and took the spokes in my hands. It was like taking the reins of a spirited horse. I felt the surging pressures of the rudder and the throb of the big diesel—if I hadn't already learned, from Washington, that the *Freya* had a diesel auxiliary, I'd have known by the stink of the exhaust blowing in over the stern.

Robin backed off, reached down, and picked up the handsome double-barreled shotgun with which she'd threatened me last night. She was wearing jeans, I noted, not the newfangled whitish kind, but the old-fashioned blue, and a navy blue turtleneck sweater. There was a bright scarf tied over her hair. Women in pants leave me cold as a rule, but she looked tall and handsome and piratical, a queen of the Spanish Main. She sat down at the side of the cockpit with her weapon across her knees, aimed at me.

"Hold her a little east of south, about 160 degrees magnetic," she said to me, and to Nick, "I'll watch him. You go help Mr. Rosten set the main. Sing out when you're ready and we'll bring her into the wind... Watch your course there, quartermaster!"

I'd let the *Freya* swing off, deliberately. Well, let's say the big schooner had wanted to go and I'd let her. She was the most boat I'd ever handled. Under other circumstances, it would have been kind of exciting to steer her—not that there wasn't a certain amount of excitement here. I glanced at the steady muzzle of the shotgun and spun the wheel the other way.

"Easy, sailor," Robin said. "Just a few spokes at a time. You can't throw an eighty-foot schooner around like a sailing dinghy. There. Hold that. Watch your compass. Meet her when she starts to swing... That's better. We'll make a helmsman of you yet, Mr. Government agent."

"Yes'm," I said. "Or should I say aye-aye."

"Matthew," she said, "or whatever your name is."

"Yes, Robin," I said.

"You should have known. You should have known I'd never encourage a cheap Chicago hood to put his hands on me."

"If that's flattery," I said, "I thank you."

"Would you have gone to bed with me? As Petroni?"

I said, "Do people have names in bed?"

"Then you would," she said. "You'd have gone that far."

"You've gone pretty far yourself, Robin," I said. "You've got a lot of people very upset."

"I guess I have." She was silent for a moment. "Like your little blonde roommate, for instance. How is the little idiot?"

"Mad at me, scared of you, and sorry for herself," I said.

Robin glanced forward to where her husband, with Nick at his side, was still working away at the nautical mysteries surrounding the base of the tall mainmast.

"So it wasn't Louis who wanted me dead, after all," she murmured. "You let me think—"

I kept my face expressionless. I saw Louis throw a glance our way, obviously wondering what we were talking about. His eyes were afraid.

"I never said it was Louis," I reminded Robin. "You were so positive, why should I argue? As Petroni, I protect my clients, lady."

She laughed. "Your client? That silly, unbalanced little girl? And you're not Petroni now, so stop calling me lady."

"Good God," I said. "I never met a bunch of people so sensitive about what they were called."

She was watching my face. "You really made a very unconvincing gangster, Matt Helm."

I grinned. "You made a very handsome mermaid, Robin Rosten."

She grimaced. "You didn't have to be so damn drastic. You didn't have to throw me in the water, and get my car stuck, and leave me to dig it out alone. You deliberately arranged for me to make a gruesome spectacle of myself in front of—" She stopped. "Oh, I see!"

"Right," I said. "It had to look good; it had to look as if I were really getting rough, to separate the sheep from the goats. It worked, didn't it? The Michaelis kid broke under the strain and showed she didn't really want anybody killed, for all her big talk. The people I was after wouldn't care who I killed; they'd killed before. We lost a man named Ames down here a while back. Remember Ames, Robin? He liked portable radios. He was also pretty good at cooking over a campfire."

"I remember a man with a radio," she said calmly. "He wasn't going under that name. He never got a chance to build a fire, if that's what he was doing on the beach at night. We thought he had something else in mind."

I looked at her for a long moment. I guess I was saying good-bye to some hope; I guess I'd been waiting for her to deny knowing anything about Ames.

"Anyway," I said, "my demonstration was convincing enough, and humiliating enough, that you didn't want any more. You dropped the respectable mask and fed me a mickey to stop me, like any movie conspirator."

She laughed. "You flatter yourself, Matt, darling, if you think your silly hoodlum antics frightened me into revealing myself."

"All right, then you got mad and lost your head; it amounts to the same thing. I got you to show your hand. You could have kept me busy for days trying to figure out if it was you I wanted, or Louis, or somebody else, but you didn't. You came right out into the open. That's what counts."

She looked at me curiously. "Why, you sound quite pleased with yourself."

"Why shouldn't I be pleased?" I asked confidently. At least I hoped I sounded confident. "As long as you were the rich and respectable Mrs. Louis Rosten, and behaved accordingly, I couldn't do much except harass you a bit, hoping you'd betray yourself—*if* you were the one I was after. Now I know you are; I've even got you to stick your neck out." I glanced at her. "It's a real pretty neck; it's going to hurt me to use the axe. But that's the way the stick floats, as the old mountain men used to say. Do you know what my boss said when he sent me on this job?"

"No." Her voice had hardened. "What did he say?"

"We were talking in Washington, only a few days ago," I said. "The chief told me, 'There are some people not forty miles from here who have to be taught not to monkey with the buzz saw when it's busy cutting wood.'" I shook my head sadly. "You shouldn't have interfered, Robin. The man Ames was after, well, we took care of him later, overseas. So what good did it do him, your helping him get away? As for Ames himself, you amateurs are all alike. You get a good racket going, and then you start killing the wrong people. It's too bad. Bye, bye, Robin."

She got to her feet, facing me, with the shotgun ready. "Don't you mean bye, bye, Matthew, darling? You seem to be forgetting something." Her voice was harsh. "You seem to be forgetting who's got what. I'm the one who's got the axe, darling. Right here in my hands, if I choose to use it."

I grinned at her cockily. "Amateur, just amateur. Waving a gun and talking loudly, just like all the rest of them. Robin, I'm ashamed of you. Don't be a two-bit Borgia, honey, do it big. If you're going to shoot me, pull the trigger, for God's sake. Get blood all over your pretty teak deck. Go ahead!" I laughed. "That's what I thought! I'm a pro, Robin, I've seen a million of you, and you're all alike. You talk a swell murder, but when it comes to a cold-blood showdown—pffft. Like a toy balloon with a pin in it. Just pffft." I made a very rude noise.

Her face was tight and pale under the smooth tan. "You take some awful chances, darling. Let me tell you something: the only reason I don't kill you is that I have other plans for you. There may even come a time when you'll wish I *had* pulled the trigger!"

"Talk," I said. "Just talk. Blah, blah, blah. There's something about holding a loaded gun that gives all amateurs verbal diarrhea. Just what is this terrible fate you have in store for me?"

She started to speak angrily, and checked herself, realizing, I guess, that I'd been deliberately trying to make her lose her temper. There was a little silence, broken by a shout from Big Nick.

"Ready with the main!"

Robin glanced that way, drew a long breath, and turned back to me. "All right, sailor. Let's see what you've learned. Bring her around easy, right up into the wind."

I swung the schooner's bow around, and the two men at the mast cranked up the big mainsail by means of a winch, and ran forward to set some other sails, while two thousand square feet of canvas, more or less, danced and flapped over my head, supporting a varnished spar the size of a telephone pole: the main boom. It was the biggest timber I'd ever seen swinging loose like that, and it made me very nervous. The tall mast and the immense sail didn't add to my peace of mind.

"Aren't you kind of shorthanded to handle a boat this size under sail?" I asked. "Three people don't seem like much of a crew."

She was watching the progress of the work forward. "We'll pick up three more tonight," she said absently, not really thinking. "Well, two that can help work the ship—" She stopped, and glanced at me quickly. "Damn you!" she said. "Well, now you know."

"Yeah," I said. "The guy who can't help is named Michaelis, I suppose, the missing Norman you were

telling me about last night. I heard about him in
Washington. Well, that's none of my business until I'm
told differently." I hoped my voice sounded easy and
casual. She had to be made to think Ames was my big
concern, not Michaelis. "I suppose that's why we're
setting the sails, so that tonight we can cut the motor and
run into Mendenhall Island silently and pick him up with
his jailers. That's the place, isn't it, the one you told me
about last night?"

"Yes," she said, "that's the place, darling. I had to say
something to keep your mind off your drink."

"And after Mendenhall," I said, "where?"

She didn't answer at once. She'd stepped off to one
side so she could see clearly. "Belay, there!" she shouted.
"You've got it fouled! Slack off the peak halfway... All
clear, hoist away." Then she turned to look at me deliberately.
"We'll head out through the Chesapeake Capes. A freighter
will meet us at sea. They'll take all of you on board—you,
Matt, in place of the woman I promised them, the one you
killed. They'll be very glad to have you, I assure you...
Nick, come here. Take him below."

19

Nick closed and bolted the cabin door behind me. I stood there for a moment, frowning. By pushing hard, I'd gained some interesting information, but I'd lost something, too. I'd annoyed my dark goddess, my pirate queen, and she'd banished me from her sight. If I'd been nicer, more flattering, less inquisitive, maybe she'd have let me stay on deck. Well, there wasn't much to be accomplished there at the moment, not against Big Nick and a double-barreled shotgun. Not bare-handed…

"What is it?" Teddy Michaelis asked fearfully, sitting up in the bunk. "What did she want with you? What happened?"

I regarded her thoughtfully. Her short, pale hair was mussed and her small face was tear-streaked. She was wearing a kind of green linen romper suit, with a short-sleeved tunic and knee pants. I don't know who dreams up these cute female costumes; I'd rather not know. All she needed was a little shovel and a tin bucket with

Donald Duck on it and a sandpile to play in. As an ally in a desperate situation, she looked pretty hopeless.

A change in the schooner's motion made me reach for the dresser to steady myself. We were turning south again. The ship took a definite list to starboard as the sails filled. I sat down on the edge of the bunk beside the kid.

"Thunderbird sent you, didn't he?" I said.

"What do you mean?"

I said, "Don't try to kid me. You'd never have thought of it yourself, not in a million years—warning Mrs. Rosten, I mean. You must have spilled your guts to young Orcutt last night after leaving my hotel room. You broke down and told him how wicked and crazy you'd been, and he showed you, sternly, where your duty lay. Am I right?"

She flushed. "Well, Billy did say—"

"Sure," I said. "I suppose the two of you decided it would look better if you came alone. But the point is, he knew where you were going this morning. When you turn up missing, what do you figure he'll do?"

"Do?" Her voice was sharp. "He won't do anything. He's never done anything in his life except talk! He's just a stuffed shirt, a pompous, moralizing prig; and I told him so last night. I told him he wasn't my conscience, and if he thought I was going to humble myself in front of his snooty aunt or cousin or whatever she is—I told him I wasn't going to do anything of the kind!"

"But you did," I pointed out.

She licked her lips. She was still trying to see herself as a ruthless, conscienceless little adventuress, but her better nature was making it rough.

"Well, I—I don't know what got into me," she said defensively. "I didn't mean—when I got into the car I hadn't the slightest intention of coming. I mean, who does he think he is, lecturing me like that!" She sniffed, on the verge of tears. "It's all his fault. If it hadn't been for him, if he hadn't taken it so big, I'd never have dreamed of coming to see her this morning! I'd have been safe now instead of—" She stopped.

"I see," I said. "In other words, he *doesn't* know where you were going. So we can't expect much help from him."

She gulped, and nodded miserably. Well, I hadn't really hoped for much from young Orcutt, any more than I'd counted on somebody checking at the hotel, learning I was missing, and taking action in time. It would be hard to say what action they could take without taking a chance of interfering with the job I was supposed to do. Jean had been supposed to make it on her own; presumably the same applied to me.

"Matt," the kid said. "That's your real name, isn't it? Matt?"

"That's right. Matt Helm, agent extraordinary, at your service, ma'am."

"Extraordinary!" she said. "I don't see anything extraordinary about you, getting yourself caught here like a—like a rat in a floating trap!" She glared at me, angry again. "You fake! You—you sheep in wolf's clothing! Pretending to be a—I knew all the time there was something phony about you!"

"Sure," I said.

"Well, I did! You don't think I really meant for you to kill—you don't think I was serious, do you? I knew all the time—I was just kidding you along, for laughs!" She sniffed and rubbed her nose with her forefinger. "I'm not fooling anybody, am I? What's going to happen to us, Matt? What's that woman going to do to us?"

"Well," I said, "first of all, I gather, she's going to take us to meet a gentleman in whom you've expressed a certain interest."

She frowned. "A gentleman?"

"A scientific sort of gent, named Michaelis."

"Papa?" Her eyes became wide and round. "You mean, he's—" She stopped, afraid to say the word.

"Alive?" I said. "Oh, yes, he's alive. They wouldn't kill him; he's much too valuable. He may not be in perfect health—don't forget he's been a prisoner for some weeks—but he's undoubtedly alive."

She licked her lips, watching my face. "But—but that's wonderful, isn't it? He's alive!"

"Yeah," I said flatly. "It's wonderful, I guess."

"Matt, what's the matter? I don't understand—"

She didn't understand, and I hadn't the slightest intention of enlightening her. *The knowledge in Dr. Michaelis' head must not leave the country*, Mac had said. That was what I was here for. It looked as if I might even accomplish it, now, and the happy expression on the face of a small, screwball blonde in green rompers had nothing whatever to do with the situation, except that it would have been nice if she'd stayed on shore where she'd belonged. Of all the witnesses I might have got stuck with, as the critical moment approached, I had to find myself sharing a cabin with Michaelis' own daughter.

"It's wonderful," I said without expression. "It's marvelous, and I'm sure you'll have a heart-warming reunion with your long-lost daddy. In fact, if things go the way Mrs. Rosten hopes, you'll have lots of opportunities to talk over old times. She's planning to put us all aboard a freighter for a long sea voyage, somewhere out beyond the three-mile limit, after which I suppose she'll turn back with her schooner and head for home. How she expects to cover up afterwards, I don't know, but she's undoubtedly got some ideas on the subject, and I wouldn't be a bit surprised if they'd work. She's a very competent lady, and she's got lots of money and plenty of nerve—"

"Oh, stop talking about her!" Teddy's voice was breathless. "Who cares about her? What happens to us?"

It was a practical point of view, but before I could discuss it with her, there were footsteps in the passageway. The knock on the door was hesitant, very different from Nick's loud warning rap.

"Yes?" I said.

"Petroni—I mean Helm?" It was Louis Rosten's voice.

"Yes?"

"Stand back. Stand well back. Don't try anything."

"Sure."

The bolt slid back and the door opened. Louis checked

himself when he saw me sitting on the bunk, facing him across the narrow cabin.

"If you jump me, it won't really help you," he said weakly.

"It'll get us out of here," I said.

"And what then? I haven't got a gun for you to use. There's only one on the ship, and you know who's got that. And you can't handle Nick without a gun, nobody can. Not to mention my dear wife herself and her smoothbore artillery, which I can assure you is loaded with buckshot in both barrels."

"All right. Come in and make your pitch, whatever it is."

He slipped inside and pressed the door closed beside him. He looked kind of shrunken inside his yachting costume. Beneath the bill of his natty cap, his handsome face was drawn and haggard. I thought I could detect hangover and fear in approximately equal concentrations.

"You've got to tell me!" he said. "I've got to know; I can't stand it any more. The way she looks at me! Is she just playing cat and mouse with me? Does she know, Helm? Have you told her?"

I glanced around the cabin. "Is it safe to talk?"

"Safe? What do you mean?"

"This cabin isn't wired for sound? I've known rooms not too far from here that were."

He shook his head quickly. "Oh, no. No, there's no microphone in here, I'm sure. There's nothing like that aboard. I'd have seen it. Well, Helm, or whatever your real name is? Have you told her? Does she know?"

Teddy, crouching on the bunk by my side, looked at him curiously. "Does who know what?" she asked.

"Mr. Rosten would like to know if his wife has been informed that, believing me to be a Chicago hoodlum, he hired me to kill her."

Teddy gasped. "You mean—you mean, he, too!" She giggled half-hysterically, and clapped her hand to her mouth.

I said, "Oh, yes, the homicide business was booming there for a while. I thought I was even going to get to collect a little from the lady for killing her husband, but that deal fell through. She was just stringing me along." I turned to Rosten. "She hasn't been enlightened by me, and to the best of my knowledge, she doesn't know. She had strong suspicions last night that it was you who hired me, but Miss Michaelis' confession this morning apparently got you off the hook. It still hasn't occurred to your wife that two people might have had the same idea simultaneously. Of course, the thought might come to her at any moment—independently or otherwise."

He stiffened. "That's a threat!"

"Yeah," I said. "That's a threat, little man. I'm in a very tough spot and I love company. I can make things just as tough for you, simply by opening my mouth."

He was used to having me bully him as Lash Petroni: he was already broken in. He wilted instantly.

"I know," he said. "I know, I've been a fool. It was a crazy idea. But I had to do something, and it seemed like the only way. It was hopeless to try to reason with her. I couldn't make her stop. We were getting in deeper and deeper. She'd forced me to help her and a man had been killed——Nick killed him, but we were all there. I didn't dare go to the authorities. I was too deeply involved; I'd lose everything if it all came out. I thought if—if she'd just die, quietly, maybe things would settle down and nobody would ever find out."

"Let's clear this up," I said. "Your wife is just about the last person I'd pick for an enemy agent. Just what the hell is she after, helping subversives to escape from the country and kidnaping people? What's she getting out of all this?"

He hesitated. We listened to the water rushing past the ship's side. There was a steady vibration from the big diesel.

"It's a little hard to explain," Louis said. "She's mad, of course, quite insane. She should be in an institution."

"Skip the diagnosis. Just give us the symptoms. What form does this madness take?"

"Well," he said, "she has declared war on the United States of America." There was a brief silence, broken by a startled giggle from Teddy. Rosten glanced at the kid, and looked back to me, challengingly. "I told you. She's crazy. First it was the bridge, you see—"

"The bridge?"

"Yes, she had a model dairy farm north of town. I don't know why she bothered with it, it didn't make much money, but it meant a great deal to her. Didn't I tell you?"

"You didn't, but she did," I said. "Go on."

"They condemned a right of way through it for the approaches to the bridge. She fought them through the courts, every step of the way, but lost. Of course, she got adequate compensation, but she couldn't see it that way. That was years ago, right after the war, but she never forgot it. And then they took Mendenhall. I told you about that. I told you she went down with a gun to hold them off. Well, she changed her mind before there was any actual shooting. She came back home. I've never seen her like that, absolutely livid, furious. That was when she—" He paused.

"Declared war?" I murmured.

"Yes. She said, if that was the way they wanted it, that was damn well the way they could have it. She could get just as rough as any lace-pants bureaucrat in Washington. They'd damn well wish they'd thought twice before they tangled with Robin Orcutt Rosten. That was how it started. She found some men with unsavory connections, I don't know how; communist agents—"

Teddy stirred. "But hasn't it occurred to Mrs. Rosten what will happen to her and her property if those people ever get into power?"

Rosten laughed shortly. "I tried to make that point. My dear wife says she'll worry about the dreadful reds if and when the time comes. She says she knows from bitter experience what happened to her under the people who are actually in power now. They took her land, she says, and she has to hire batteries of high-priced lawyers and tax experts to keep them from taking her money, too, and giving it away to people who are too lazy to work and nations that are too stupid to—Well, you can complete the argument for yourselves. She says it came to her when she was down at Mendenhall preparing to stand them off with her shotgun: instead of peppering a few stupid yokels in soldier suits, she was going to do some damage where it really counted. She might not win, but those bureaucrats in Washington would know they'd been in a fight, by God!" He grimaced. "I told you. She's insane."

"Yeah," I said. "Insane."

He was right of course. The lady was cracked; she had to be. And still, there was a kind of romantic appeal in the idea of a lone woman in a sailboat setting out to wreak vengeance on the forces of progress: the taxes, the bridges, the military installations. Even if you didn't agree with her point of view, you could have admired her—or at least her courage—if she'd only been a little more careful, or patriotic, about picking her associates; if she'd refrained from kidnaping and killing people. I stopped that line of thought, as something changed around us. Aft, the diesel went silent; the engine vibrations stopped. I glanced out the porthole. The schooner was rushing along with apparently undiminished speed. I looked at Rosten.

"What does that mean?"

"My wife seems to have shut down the auxiliary," he said. "The wind has been rising steadily; she must figure we'll do well enough from now on under sail alone."

I said, "There's a storm to the south of us, I understand."

"A little more than just a storm, Mr. Helm," he said, rather pompously. "There's a hurricane off the Carolinas; but it's veering out to sea, according to the latest weather reports. However, we'll get the fringes of it before the night is over. I hope you have a strong stomach. The *Freya* is seaworthy enough to take anything we're apt to run into, but she can get quite active in a blow." He laughed, with a hint of malice. "She looks like a pretty big boat, doesn't she? I think you'll find her looking somewhat smaller shortly."

I said, "If things get good and rough, we'll have a better chance for a break. The timing will have to be right. Are you willing to help?"

He hesitated, and avoided answering directly. "Anything you do had better be done before we reach Mendenhall tonight," he said uneasily. "There'll be two men bringing Dr. Michaelis aboard—you heard about that; I heard my wife telling you. These men are trained professionals, like you. After they get on board, you won't stand a chance against all of them."

Teddy started to speak angrily. I put my hand on her knee. "I think we'd better wait for her daddy to get aboard, if we can," I said, and tried not to notice the quick look of gratitude she gave me.

Rosten said, "But that's ridiculous! We've got to act while we—" He checked himself, confused.

I said, "So now it's we. Thanks."

He ignored that. "—while we have the advantage of numbers, at least. Let me get on deck. I'll leave the door unlocked. I'll station myself where I can reach the shotgun. When you slip on deck, forward, and create a disturbance, I'll grab the gun and we'll have them."

It sounded beautifully simple and easy. I had to act as if I was tempted by the idea. To tell the truth, I was.

"Well—"

Teddy asked quickly, "What about Papa?"

"After we get control of the schooner," Rosten said, "we can radio the authorities and have him rescued. He's being held in the wine cellar of the old Orcutt mansion on the island. My wife discovered it as a child, playing among the ruins. It was her secret, and she covered the entrance with brush and rubble so no one else would find it. No one has, not even the Marines. They don't really use the island for anything; they just keep people off because it's right in line with a small-arms range they have on shore. The men holding Dr. Michaelis have plenty of supplies in there, and a rubber boat, and a portable radio receiver—"

"Ouch," I said. "What makes you think they won't be listening when we start broadcasting for official help?"

Rosten said impatiently, "That's a risk we'll have to run. Anyway, even if they're warned, how far can they get in a little rubber boat on a stormy night? Our first concern is to take over the *Freya* while we have a chance."

Teddy said hotly, "Maybe it's *your* first concern, but—"

"All right," he said irritably. "We won't use the radio. We'll land somewhere and find a telephone."

"Ha-ha," she said. "How many places along the Bay can you land an eighty-foot schooner drawing ten feet of water, and who's going to take her in with a gale blowing? You?"

He said stiffly, "I can handle the *Freya*, Miss Michaelis."

"Yes, I've seen you! You put us aground in the James River in broad daylight, the time Papa and I came cruising with you all. It took high tide and a couple of powerboats to get us off, remember? If you do that here, Papa dies or vanishes again." She turned to me, breathlessly. "Matt, you're a government man. You know Papa is an important man, you said so. You think we'd better wait, don't you?"

I didn't trust Louis Rosten very far, and I didn't want him thinking I considered Dr. Michaelis particularly important, in case he should talk out of turn.

I said, "Well, rescuing Dr. Michaelis isn't strictly speaking in my department—"

"There's an alternative," Rosten said quickly. "We take over the ship and sail to the rendezvous ourselves. The two men with Dr. Michaelis won't be expecting trouble when they come on board. We should be able to overpower them easily."

The kid asked quickly, "And what makes you think you can bring us into Mendenhall Bay in the dark, no better than you navigate? I know I couldn't. Do you even know the right place? What if there's a special signal? There must be some kind of a signal to bring them out. Do you know what it is?"

I was watching Louis while she threw her objections at him. Maybe they were valid and maybe they weren't, and I could see it didn't matter in the least, because Louis had no intention of effecting a rescue at the slightest risk to himself. I could see his mind working as clearly as if his skull had been transparent. He wasn't brave, but he wasn't stupid, either. He had the essential point clearly in mind: the fact that when we finished taking over the ship according to his plan, he would be the man holding the shotgun.

Once we'd helped him dispose of his wife and Nick, he was thinking, he wouldn't really need us any more, not even to work the schooner. At the worst, he could get the big sails down somehow, turn on the engine, and go where he pleased. Less drastically, he could force us to do the safe and prudent thing, and to hell with Dr. Michaelis—or so he thought.

Actually, in his hands, a shotgun probably wasn't quite the magic wand he believed it to be; but the sly, unreliable look in his eyes was the important thing, from my point of view. Going after Michaelis involved too many imponderables, anyway. I couldn't afford to let myself be dazzled by any glittering, gold-plated shortcuts. There was only one reasonably certain way for me to carry out my mission here, and that was to let Michaelis be brought to me.

"We'll wait," I said. "We'll let them come on board."

Rosten said angrily, "You're in no position to dictate—"

I got up. He stopped talking and stepped back warily. I said, "There are three of us. You've been outvoted."

"If I decide not to help you—"

I said, "You've pretty well got to do something, with us or without us, before your wife catches onto you. If you want to try it on your own, go ahead. You'll have two shots, if you get your hands on the gun. Let me give you a little professional advice, Rosten: once you make your move, don't hesitate for a fraction of a second. Don't make any speeches; don't strike any poses; just grab the gun and shoot. Take Mrs. Rosten with the first barrel if she's closer; but be sure you get Nick with the second, because he won't give you time to reload. It will be kind of gory. A shotgun makes a hell of a mess at close range. But you don't care about that. What's the matter?"

He was looking kind of green. "I—what do you want me to do? To help, I mean?"

It wouldn't have been diplomatic to gloat over his surrender. I said, "You'd better bolt the door when you leave now, but I'll expect it to get unbolted quietly right after the passengers come aboard, before we're clear of the land and everybody starts relaxing and looking around."

"All right. I'll try." He didn't sound happy.

"Then I'd like an adjustable crescent wrench, five or six inches long, as soon as you can manage to smuggle it in here. You can pick one up in the engine room or somewhere, can't you, and slip it inside your shirt? A pair of pliers might work, or a small Stillson. Can do?"

A suspicious look came to his face. He glanced at the porthole. "If you think you're going to slip out through that when we get close to shore, and leave me holding the bag—"

"Hell, man, I can't swim fifty yards in calm water, and who's going to open that thing with a little six-inch crescent, the way they have it bolted down? Just get me the wrench, huh? And now you'd better get out of here before you're missed and she sends Nick looking for you."

He left, looking like a man keeping a date for his own hanging. After the door had closed behind him, Teddy turned to look at me. Her eyes were bright. She hesitated; then she grabbed my arm and pulled me down beside her so she could kiss me on the ear.

"You were wonderful! I—I'm sorry about all the mean things I said to you, Matt!"

"Sure," I said.

"It's going to be all right, isn't it? With his help—"

"Sure," I said. "It's going to be fine."

"I—I'll always be grateful. If—if we get out of this, I'll show you how grateful I am," she murmured, clinging to my arm.

"Cut it out," I said. "Don't strain my self-control. I might get ideas and rape you right here."

That brought a startled little giggle from her. After a moment, she said, "Well, go ahead. There isn't much else to do in this dismal box of a cabin, and we won't reach Mendenhall until way after dark." She pecked at my ear. "Go ahead. If you want to."

I turned to look at her. After a moment, her eyes wavered and color came into her face. She was being terribly wicked again; she was being grownup and sophisticated; she was bluffing. It would have been interesting to determine how far she'd carry it, strictly as a scientific project, of course; but this was hardly the time for irrelevant experiments. Besides, at the moment she had no more physical attraction for me than a plastic doll. In fact, I'd have given a great deal to be able to replace her with a doll—a doll with blind glass eyes, and no capacity for emotion or memory.

"Cut it out, Teddy," I said shortly.

"Well, you're the one who brought it up!" This wasn't exactly true, but I didn't challenge it. I saw relief in her eyes, and also a kind of triumph: she'd made me, an older man, back down on a matter of sex. She laughed and hugged my arm fondly. "I know it's going to be all right, I just know it!" she breathed. "You know all about these things; you'll fix it, won't you, Matt? I knew the minute I saw you that you were somebody special, somebody different from all the silly kids..."

I sat there awkwardly as she snuggled up against me and gave me the line she must have developed for entertaining her father's friends. I didn't resent it. She was just talking too much because she was scared. She had a right to be. She didn't know how different I was.

I sat there thinking about the way it was going to have to be done. I had no faith in Louis Rosten. If he came through, that was fine, but I couldn't count on him; and even if I could, I certainly couldn't count on being able to take over the schooner with his help and that of a ninety-pound girl—not against Robin Rosten, Big Nick, and two enemy pros.

I'd talked about it blithely because it was what I was expected to talk about—by Teddy, by Rosten, and by Robin herself, if her husband should decide to betray our grandiose plans to her—but it simply wasn't a reliable solution. Whatever I really did, it would have to be quick and unexpected, and it would have to take place right here in this tiny cabin.

The knowledge in Dr. Michaelis' head must not leave the country. To make sure that it didn't, the man would have to die practically the moment he was pushed in the door—assuming my luck held that far, and he was actually put in here with us. There couldn't be any hesitation or stalling around; there couldn't be any waiting to see what might or might not happen afterwards, with or without the help of Louis Rosten.

The little girl beside me nibbled affectionately at my ear. "You think I'm being silly and corny, don't you, Matt?" she murmured. "You think I'm just babbling away because I'm scared silly. Well, maybe I am, but I really do think you're—"

I felt her start and look up at the deck over our heads. The schooner was talking loudly now, driving hard southwards, creaking and groaning; but there had been another noise, something like a human cry. Teddy looked at me apprehensively. I moved my shoulders briefly. After a little, we heard sounds in the passageway.

It was Louis, of course. He'd managed to louse it up even faster than I'd expected. Nick threw him in and bolted the door again. I got down from the bunk and turned him over. His left arm didn't seem to be properly attached to his body. Teddy screamed when she saw what had happened to his face.

20

Please don't think I'm being callous, or anything, when I say it was kind of a relief. It blew away, so to speak, the cobwebs of illusion. It was tough on Louis, but he wasn't a particularly good friend of mine, and it made everything sharp and clear. We could all stop kidding each other now.

I mean, the message was plain: we were through with the phony glamor and politeness. We were through with lovely ladies in filmy peignoirs smiling seductively as they passed out the loaded highballs; we were through with the trick psychology, the slick dialogue, and all the rest of the Hollywood jazz.

Instead, we had, on deck, harsh reality in the shape of a tough woman with delusions of persecution and grandeur, in jeans, packing a shotgun, with a murderous giant to do her bidding. And below, in the swaying and weaving little steel prison of a cabin, we had some more crude reality in the form of a man with a dislocated shoulder, perhaps a cracked skull, certainly a broken nose and several missing front teeth, bleeding copiously. It was an effective antidote to dreams. We weren't going to walk out through an unbolted door and take over the schooner with a wave of the hand. Well, I hadn't ever thought we would, really.

Teddy stared in horror at the beaten man on the floor. She gagged suddenly and scrambled into the head—to use the nautical term—and was sick. I bent down and looked Louis over. I patted him around the body and found no tools or weapons of any kind. That figured. I opened his shirt and looked at his shoulder. It was dramatic. Nick had practically torn the arm off, as you'd rip a drumstick from a cold roast chicken.

What had happened was pretty obvious. Robin hadn't brought me on deck just for fun. In spite of Teddy's confession, she'd remained suspicious of her husband, and she'd had me up there to tease him. She'd let him see us talking cozily together, knowing that, if guilty, he couldn't help but wonder if I was giving him away right before his eyes. She'd known he couldn't stand the pressure; he'd have to go to me for reassurance as soon as possible.

She'd waited for him to betray himself by slipping below to talk to me. When he came back, she'd simply turned Nick loose. With his arm twisted out of its socket, Louis would have talked, all right. He would have told her everything she wanted to know, and all it had got him was a smashed face and a crack on the head. I couldn't help wondering if the brutal embellishments had been Nick's idea or Robin's. I wouldn't have laid bets either way. She was no longer the warm and lovely woman I'd held in my arms; but then, that woman had never really existed…

There wasn't anything I could do for the arm except lash it to Louis' side with his shirt so it wouldn't flop around when I heaved him into the bunk. He paid no attention. He'd been hit hard enough, undoubtedly, to have a concussion; he might even die. I looked into the cubicle next door. The kid had pulled herself together, but she was having trouble pumping out the plumbing. I gave her a hand.

As we struggled with the machinery, the schooner took a sharp list to starboard, and solid green water sluiced briefly across the outside of the smaller porthole above the john. I had to grab Teddy and brace myself to keep both of us from being thrown into the pipes and valves.

I said, "Hell, are we sinking?"

She giggled in spite of herself. "Haven't you ever been on a sailboat before? They all sail on their sides, silly. It's just getting a little gusty out there, and the wind seems to've hauled more abeam." Her amusement faded abruptly. "Matt, now there's nobody to help! What are we going to do?"

I knew what I was going to do, but I could hardly tell her about it. I had no choice now, if I'd ever had any.

She clung to me desperately. "What's going to happen to us?" she breathed. "Where is that woman sending Papa and the rest of us? You didn't tell me. If we can't get away before she puts up on board that ship, what will happen to us?"

If she didn't want to know, she shouldn't ask. I said, "My impression is, we'll be taken overseas to a country where there are some specialists waiting to torture hell out of us—that is, unless there are facilities and experts on the freighter."

Her eyes were wide and shocked. "*Torture?*"

"Torture," I said. "Don't be naïve. Take a look at Louis, for a practical illustration of what happens to people who know things other people want to know."

"But—"

"Your daddy has some very special information," I said, "and I happen to be connected with a government agency that has aroused a lot of curiosity over there. They had a lady scheduled to take the trip voluntarily, but she died. Well, you know. You were at the motel that night."

Teddy glanced at me. "Did you really kill her, Matt?"

"Let's not go into that," I said. "It's complicated and irrelevant. Anyway, I've been drafted as a replacement. I'm sure there are long lists of questions just waiting to be asked both Dr. Michaelis and me, and all kinds of fancy drugs and devices to make sure we're properly cooperative."

Teddy licked her lips, looking up at me. "But—but I don't know anything!" she cried. "What do they want with me?"

"Well, you annoyed Mrs. Rosten," I said. "You were a contributing factor in getting her all wet, remember. And then you had the bad judgment to show up just at sailing time; and as I told you, your daddy knows something quite important; and one of the best ways to get information out of a stubborn man is to go to work on somebody he happens to be very fond of."

"You mean—you mean they'd hurt me just to get him to talk?" She glanced at me, and looked away. "I'm sorry. That's a pretty selfish attitude, I guess. I just—I've never been in anything like this before."

I helped her out of the head, wishing she wouldn't keep showing flashes of something kind of honest and likable. I mopped some blood off the cabin floor and helped her get settled there with a pillow, since she didn't want to share the bed with Louis, who was breathing in a funny way and showed no signs of regaining consciousness. I tried to make myself comfortable, sitting on the dresser. It was the only vacant space left. From there, I could look out through the cabin porthole, but the only view was of white-topped waves that occasionally washed up against the glass.

They got higher as the afternoon passed, and the motion got more violent. I wasn't surprised when at last Teddy got up quickly and vanished into the head. After all, she'd already done it once; she'd have it in mind. She came out looking pale and miserable and curled up with her pillow, but presently she had to rush in there again. This time she stayed so long I finally went in after her.

She was really in bad shape, too sick to give a damn about the humiliation of having me see her and help her. It was a long nightmare afternoon, and it didn't get much better after it turned into night, with Louis making strange breathing noises in the berth and the kid deathly seasick in the john. It didn't seem quite fair. What I was going to do to Michaelis was bad enough without my having to prepare for it by holding his little girl's head and wiping her chin.

I got her out of the head at last, and she was curled up on the floor, moaning, a small, bedraggled ball of misery, when the motion of the schooner changed quite perceptibly. I switched off the electric light by the dresser and looked out through the porthole. Out in the darkness, the waves, that had been marching off at an angle to the schooner's course, were moving right along with us; we'd changed direction. There were footsteps overhead, and the sounds of ropes being hauled through blocks. I slid off the dresser and bent over the kid.

"Snap out of it, Teddy," I said. "Something's happening. Brief me."

I had to shake her a couple of times before she'd let me help her to her feet. She looked out the porthole and listened. "We're heading straight down wind," she said. "I think we're about to jibe."

"Isn't that dangerous?"

I'd seen it happen on a small scale, years ago, when one of our group had accidentally jibed a twenty-five-footer in training. The guy had been careless, the wind had got behind the mainsail, and the boom—a toothpick compared to the *Freya*'s massive spar—had slashed across the cockpit like a scythe; in an instant, the boat had been lying flat on its side, half full of water.

Teddy laughed at me. She seemed to be feeling better, suddenly; perhaps because the motion had lessened, now that we were running straight before the wind.

"Oh, an uncontrolled jibe could dismast the ship, but with that woman at the wheel and Nick to handle the mainsheet and backstays—"

"What's a sheet? I forget."

She glanced at me over her shoulder. "You don't really know very much, do you?"

I said, "I haven't been puking all over the damn boat, either, small stuff. Let's not get into a comparison of our seagoing abilities, huh? What's a sheet?"

"The mainsheet is the line—rope to you—controlling the mainsail." Her voice was stiff. "To jibe under control, or wear ship as they used to call it, Nick's got to get the sail sheeted flat aft so it can't swing, and the starboard backstay set up taut; then Mrs. Rosten will bring the stern through the wind… There!"

There was a lurch, and I felt the schooner heel over to the left—excuse me, to port. Above us, blocks squealed and spars creaked; the whole ship seemed to sigh, taking the strain of the masts and rigging a different way.

"Now we're on the starboard track," the kid said. "Nick's cast off the port backstay and is slacking off on the mainsheet… You didn't have to say that!"

"Say what?"

She turned to face me. I could see her vaguely in the yellow glow from the bathroom, where the light was still on. She had a pale, rumpled, wrung-out look; but she was focusing again. Her voice was shrill.

"Just because I don't have the stomach of a goat, like some people!"

"Easy, kid," I said. "I didn't mean—"

"Don't call me kid," she gasped. "I'm twenty-two years old and I'm not a kid and I know you think I'm an absolute fool, the way I've behaved. Theodora the Terrible, the ruthless murderess who can't bear the thought of blood, the irresistible siren who doesn't really want to be touched, the nautical expert who can't even keep her lunch down when it blows. Well, how would you like to be a cute little female Tom Thumb all your life? I'm not a toy, damn it, I'm a person; but try to make people believe it! Just try!" She drew a long, ragged breath. "Here we go again!"

There was again that odd stillness as the schooner came dead before the wind, and the lurch as the sails swung across and filled on the new tack.

"We must be maneuvering inshore," Teddy said. Her voice was suddenly calm again. She looked out. "I can't see anything. I bet they're sweating up there, just the two of them, working a boat this size in shallow water. I hope that woman knows what she's doing. If she puts us aground in this wind, she'll break the ship in two. We'd drown in here before anybody—Matt," she whispered, turning. "Matt, I'm sorry. Be nice to me. I'm so damn scared!"

It was the moment for me to take her into my arms and smooth the matted fair hair back from her small face and kiss her and tell her everything was going to be all right, even if I didn't mean it. It was what she wanted me to do, and I was damned if I'd do it. She at least could have stayed sick; she didn't have to get up and explain her lousy little psyche to me, as if I cared.

Abruptly, the schooner turned left for what seemed an hour, leaning over hard; then it came upright. The sound of flapping canvas reached us from above. I looked at Teddy.

"We've rounded up into the wind," she said. Her voice was strained. "They must be—taking somebody on board."

Something thumped against the side of the ship. We heard footsteps overhead. Suddenly Robin Rosten's voice was speaking in the passageway.

"Straight ahead. Not in there, that's the head—bathroom to you. It's the cabin to starboard. No, no, on your right, you lubber. Throw him in and let's get topside and give Nick a hand before we drift onto the shoals."

The man who opened the door had a seamed, whiskery face and a meaty nose. Remove the whiskers, and it was a face I'd seen in the files, but I couldn't recall the name that went with it. Well, I'd figured he'd be somebody reasonably familiar. Robin had got my code name from the conversation I'd had with Jean; but the name Matthew Helm hadn't been mentioned in that hotel room. She had to have got that from somebody who knew the two names went together.

He'd seen my face somewhere, too, and he was glad to see it again. "Mister Helm," he said. "How nice to make your acquaintance. I have been looking forward to it. You are not as pretty as the lady we were expecting, the one with such a deplorable fondness for liquor, but I'm sure my superiors will not complain…"

"Stow it, Loeffler," Robin said, behind him. "Never mind the corny dialogue. Just shove in the doctor and secure the door."

"Secure? Ah, you mean fasten—"

The man called Loeffler—which wasn't the name we had him filed under—got a grip on the sagging figure supported between him and Robin, and propelled him forward for me to catch. The door closed, and I was standing there with Dr. Norman Michaelis in my arms, the man I'd come to silence. I remembered Mac's words clearly: *How to achieve this result is left entirely to the discretion of the agent on the spot. Do you understand?*

I'd understood perfectly then, and I understood just as well now. It was a moment of triumph, in a way. I'd broken discipline and disobeyed orders to get here. I'd played gangster and let myself be drugged and imprisoned. I might never get out alive, but at least my job was finished. Jean's job was finished. I was here, and so was the subject I'd come to find. The rest, for a man of my training, was just a technical detail.

21

"Is he—going to be all right?"

That was Teddy, behind me, trying to get a look at her parent as I put him into the bunk beside Louis. It was a damn fool question. Probably none of us were going to be all right. Certainly Dr. Norman Michaelis wasn't, not if I could help it.

He looked about as you'd expect a man to look after being imprisoned for a lengthy interval in a ruined cellar. He seemed to be wearing slacks, a sport shirt, and rubber-soled shoes. I remembered that he'd vanished while out sailing. The mechanics of it had never been explained to me, and didn't really matter. I wasn't about to wake him up to ask him.

The clothes were filthy, his hair was long and tangled, and he had a beard like a hermit. He looked half-starved to boot. He was out cold.

"What's the matter with him?" Teddy wailed. "Why doesn't he wake up?"

I said, "They've got him under drugs. It's the lazy man's way of keeping a prisoner quiet. Besides, the right drugs used long enough affect the will to resist. I guess they were softening him up for the interrogation experts."

My voice sounded dry and pedantic and far away. It would have been such an easy job if I'd been alone with him; it would have been over already. He was drugged, weakened by exposure and hunger; it would have been no more trouble than blowing out a candle.

His lips moved. "AUDAP? I don't know anything about—no, no, I won't tell—you can't make me tell!"

He was wrong. They could make him tell. They could make almost any man tell almost anything—unless the man were dead. I thought of the odd-looking nuclear submarines with their incredible loads of destruction upon which, Mac had been told by the Navy, depended the safety of the nation and the peace of the world. Even if the picture was a little exaggerated—I'd never yet met a military man who was entirely objective about the importance of his own service—the decision wasn't mine to make. I had my orders.

I stuck my elbow into the kid crowding against me. "Get over by the porthole, Teddy. Tell me if you can see anything. Brief me."

"But—"

"Snap into it. I'll look after him." I'd look after him, all right.

She moved away reluctantly. I was aware of her leaning forward to wipe at the glass—and there was my

chance. The little death pill was in my hand. I hated to
part with it, I might need it myself pretty soon, but it was
the best way. All I had to do was slip it into his mouth and
make him swallow. She'd never know. He'd simply have
died in his drugged sleep, as far as she was concerned.

Her voice hit me like a sonic boom. "We've turned
back north; we've got the island off the starboard. We're
close-hauled, beating out of Mendenhall Bay. We'll have
to tack as soon as we're clear of the island to make open
water. I hope that woman's got her bearings straight. We
can't have much room to play around in here, in a boat
this size."

My voice still came from far away. "Why would Mrs.
Rosten come clear in here, in the first place, instead of
picking them up on the seaward side of the island, where
we had plenty of room and couldn't be seen from shore?"

"Don't be silly, she had to get in the lee to bring them
aboard. They'd never have been able to get a rubber boat
out to us seaward, not against this wind. There must be
a mile of breakers on that side tonight." Teddy leaned
forward. "We're still holding on; we've got a ways to go
yet before we can come about and clear the island on the
port tack…"

I looked at the man on the bunk. *Stop stalling, you
spineless jerk!* I told myself. I leaned forward and made
a show of drawing back the eyelid to look at the eye, like
a TV doctor. I picked up the wrist to check the pulse. I
dropped the wrist and leaned forward again to put my
hand to his mouth. Teddy spoke behind me.

"What are you doing, Matt? What are you giving him?"

I didn't even jump. I guess I'd known it wouldn't work out right. Maybe I hadn't even wanted it to work out right. But it was all of a pattern, I thought grimly: the woman who'd died when she wasn't supposed to and the man who was alive five minutes after he should have been dead. I should, of course, have done it the instant they threw him into my arms, as I'd planned, and to hell with who saw what. I might even have got away with it, then.

I turned my head slowly. "Benzedrine," I said. "To bring him around."

She was frowning at me. I don't put much stock in feminine intuition; she'd have been a real dope if she hadn't sensed something, after the fumble-witted stalling I'd done.

"Let me see it," she said in an odd little voice, and I showed it to her on the palm of my hand. She asked, "How do you happen to have—"

"Hell, we always carry bennies to keep us awake on a tough job."

"But are you sure that's the right thing to give him?"

Her voice had an absent sound, as if she wasn't really interested in the question she was asking. She was still frowning, not at the pill, but at me. Her blue eyes were narrow and wondering. She knew that something was wrong, terribly wrong, but the idea that had come into her mind was too far-out to put into words... She did it without a hint of warning. She just grabbed the pill out of my hand and started bringing it to her mouth; and I swung without thinking, slapping it away before it reached her lips. I guess I'd have done the same thing even if I'd had time to think.

The pill rolled away across the teak floor, and then came back towards us as the *Freya* heeled over. It reminded me, somehow, of one of the pearls from Jean's broken necklace. I got up and picked it up. I went into the john, dropped it into the toilet, and pumped it out of sight. When I came back, she was still standing stiffly by the bed.

"No!" she said breathlessly. "Stay away! Don't come near him!"

She was staring at me as if she had never seen me before. Perhaps she hadn't. "You—were going to *kill* him!" she whispered.

I laughed. "You've got murder on the brain, small stuff. I told you, it was a benny."

"Then why didn't you let me swallow it?"

"You're crazy enough without being hopped up on benzedrine. Now cut out the melodramatics, Teddy, and—"

"That's why you wanted us to wait until he came aboard, so you could kill him. So he couldn't tell anybody—and I thought you were being so brave and generous!"

I said, "For the love of Pete, cut it out! Don't throw a wingding on me now."

She said fiercely, "You'll have to kill me, too! You know that, don't you? If anything happens to him, anything at all, you'll have to kill me, too!"

I looked at her grimly, wondering what I'd done to be

punished by having to deal with this unpredictable little
bundle of cowardice and courage, of nonsense and sense.

I said wearily, "It will be a pleasure to assassinate you,
Peewee, as soon as we're out of this. Just call on me any
time. But right now, will you get to that damn window
and tell me—"

"Porthole," she said mechanically. They'll never let
you call any part of a ship by the wrong name, even if the
bucket's sinking under you.

"All right, porthole!" I said. "Now snap out of it.
Nobody's going to touch your old man. At least I'm not.
So get over there—"

The *Freya* changed course sharply. I heard the thunder
of flapping canvas overhead as she came to an even keel.
Teddy glanced at me warily and darted to the porthole.

"We're coming about!" she said. She sounded shocked.
"I don't understand! Mrs. Rosten can't possibly hope to
lay a course out past the island yet, with the wind in this
quarter. She'll put us aground on—what's that?"

A vibration went through the schooner's hull. For a
moment, I thought we'd struck bottom; and I saw the
same thought in Teddy's eyes. We stared at each other
dumbly, forgetting everything else. The vibration settled
down to a strong, steady rumble that shook the lights and
made the door rattle. I drew a long breath.

"She's just started up the mill, that's all," I said.

"We're still swinging!" Teddy said, bewildered. "She's
bearing off before the wind, back into Mendenhall Bay."
Her small face lighted up. She whirled to grab me by the

arm. "Matt, we're saved! There must be somebody out there, heading her off, to make her turn back like that. She's started the auxiliary because it doesn't matter who hears her now, don't you see? But she's trapped inside the island. They're bound to catch her!"

We leaned forward together, peering out. There was nothing to be seen except darkness and water—black, foam-flecked water, hissing past. We were traveling faster than we'd gone all day.

"She's really pouring the oil to that diesel," I said. "Just how far can she run in this direction before piling up?" Teddy didn't answer. I glanced at her, and saw that her elation had faded as suddenly as it had come. Her face was quite white. "What's the matter, kid?" I asked.

Teddy licked her lips. "She's going to try the channel. She—she'll kill us all!"

"Channel?" I said. "What channel?" Then I remembered that Robin herself had said something about a tidal channel between the island and the mainland. She'd also mentioned a mile of shoals, I recalled.

Teddy said dully, "It's very simple. She's just going to take ten feet of draft through an eight-foot channel at fourteen knots, that's all. Listen! They're running up the foresail again. They had it down for a while."

"Translate," I said. "Never mind the damn sail. What's this about eight feet and ten feet?"

"Well, the channel's supposed to be eight feet at mean low water. If the tide is high, she may have ten or even twelve, but even so—"

"So she *could* make it?"

"No, you don't understand!" she protested. "It's a narrow channel; it isn't dredged; it isn't buoyed; it just goes where the tide goes. It changes with every storm. It says eight feet on the chart, but that doesn't mean anything. There could be a sandbar clear across it tomorrow—or tonight!"

"Skip the could-be's," I said. "Obviously she thinks she's got a chance or she wouldn't try it. But suppose she does, what does it get her? I mean, this is just a glorified sailboat, after all. You said fourteen knots just now, and she's giving it everything she's got—sail, power, everything. Right?"

"Yes, but—"

"But, hell!" I said. "I don't know much about boats, but I do know that fourteen knots is nothing, even on the water. A knot is only a fraction over a mile per hour, isn't it? A fast twin-screw cruiser can do forty and better, can't it? We've been spotted and somebody's chasing us, obviously. If it's the Marines or the Coast Guard, they're going to have something reasonably speedy, aren't they? They aren't apt to be patrolling the area in a rowboat. Even if Mrs. Rosten makes it out through the channel at a lousy fourteen knots, she'll be run down in a couple of miles, won't she?"

"You don't understand!" Teddy said plaintively. There seemed to be a lot I didn't understand. "There's a gale blowing out there already; it will be worse before morning. You heard Louis. On a reasonably calm day, any little outboard motorboat could catch us, but the *Freya* is a seagoing schooner, Matt! She's built to stay out and take it. Very few powerboats are, certainly not here on the Bay. Nobody's going to chase us at forty knots in this weather, or fourteen knots, either. Not out past the shelter of Mendenhall Island, they aren't. In a wind like this, no small craft is going to catch an eighty-foot schooner on a reach, as long as the masts stay in her."

"I see," I said. "So once the lady gets clear of the land, she's home free."

Teddy nodded. "Unless the Navy gets a destroyer out of Norfolk to look for her; and with the tail end of a hurricane to hide in, she has a very good chance of slipping out to sea, anyway, radar or no radar. Getting back home again after the weather has cleared will be another matter, but that won't help us a bit." She glanced at the porthole and gulped. "That is, assuming she can get us through that silly little channel. If she can't she'll drown us all!"

"I knew I should have learned to swim better," I said.

She looked at me for a moment, and remembered she didn't trust me, and drew away a little. "It doesn't matter much does it? We aren't any of us going to swim very far, in here with the door locked."

The schooner gave a sudden lurch, throwing us against the bunk. It wasn't anything, just a gust of wind; she rose again, shuddering and vibrating, driving hard towards the unseen channel ahead, fleeing the unknown threat astern. I had a mental picture of my cruel pirate queen at the wheel. Big Nick would be forward as lookout, maybe out on the bowsprit, scanning the water ahead. Loeffler and his unidentified associate would be huddled in whatever shelter they could find against the spray, commending their souls to some Marxist god, unless they were better sailors than I thought...

The kid did something that caught my attention, I didn't quite know why. She'd been bending over the bunk to help her father, who'd slid down on top of Louis, to leeward; and suddenly she'd done something quick and sneaky. Now she was turning away guiltily, hiding something. I grabbed her and swung her around. Her hand came up, striking at me with something, in a panicky way. I parried the blow and got the thing away from her. It was a rusty wrench.

22

I stared at the wrench for a moment. Then I looked at Teddy, who was rubbing her bruised wrist.

"It was—in Louis' sock," she said, glaring at me. "You didn't have to break my arm!"

I didn't bother to ask why she'd tried to hide it. The answer was in her face. She'd been going to wait until my back was turned and slug me with it, after which, presumably, she'd have rescued Papa somehow, from me as well as from the people on deck.

I looked at Louis. The rolling around had worked his pants leg up towards the knee, but of course I should have looked there when I first searched him. I'd had hours to go over him thoroughly, but I'd taken for granted there wasn't anything to find. I'd assumed that he'd never really meant to get us anything useful, that he hadn't had time, or even if he'd got it, that he'd told all about it and had it taken away from him.

I'd made the mistake that's so easy to make in this

business: I'd sold a guy short because I didn't trust him or like him. Louis had given me what I'd asked for. He'd even kept quiet about it through a brutal third degree. I'd passed it up because I'd been too smart to really look for it.

Well, it was no time to start counting my shortcomings; that would have to wait until I had a week or two to spare. The funny thing was that I felt pretty good, suddenly. I looked at the kid, standing there defiantly, and at Dr. Michaelis, lying in the bunk behind her; and I knew that I'd had it, I was through, and it felt fine. I knew I wouldn't have killed him if he'd had the secret of the universe locked inside his unkempt head.

I was remembering what Mac had said happened to men whose business allowed them to kill and get away with it. I was remembering Jean dying in my arms, and the hasty knife going into Alan, and the careless way I'd almost put a bullet through young Orcutt's head. Mac had been right, and Klein, the psychiatrist. It was time I got the hell out of the lousy racket...

First, of course, I had to get the hell out of here. I looked at the wrench. It was no beauty, but it was in working order. I pulled off my belt. The rectangular buckle wasn't as big as I'd have liked—Lash Petroni hadn't been the type for wide, cowboy-style belts—but under the leather covering it was of hardened steel with sharp edges, built to come in handy in emergencies.

I snapped the buckle from the belt, and peeled the leather from the buckle. The pencil from the coat pocket of my Petroni suit went through the hole in the buckle for leverage, and I had a reasonable facsimile of a screwdriver. Teddy was watching me with a kind of fearful respect, as if expecting me to produce a pocket model ray gun, or a Dick Tracy wrist radio. Her attitude annoyed me. She wasn't really very bright, or she'd have been asking why I hadn't done all this two hours ago.

"Put up the side of that bunk so our patients don't fall out if things get rugged," I said. "Then keep an eye to the porthole and an ear to the door, if you can manage. If you see anything out there, let me know. If you hear anybody coming, let me know. Okay?"

"Yes, Matt," she said, but I noted she didn't get too far from the bunk until I'd made my way past her into the bathroom.

It still looked as interesting as it had when I first cased the joint for possible tools or weapons—that husky lever, I mean, the one that ran the plumbing. It was attached to the machinery in two places: through a pivot at the bottom, and a rod about halfway up that actuated a kind of piston when you pushed and pulled. There were two paint-choked screws to be extracted from two paint-choked nuts. It took me about ten minutes to do the job, and I had a piece of steel about two feet long with a shiny brass handle.

I also had some bleeding knuckles and an incipient case of seasickness: the kid had messed up the place pretty badly, and the schooner was by no means standing still. In fact, it seemed damn close to capsizing as it roared along, but I wasn't taking time out to ask damn fool questions.

I figured, if we were really going over, my little nautical expert would come in and give me the word.

When I made my way back into the cabin, she was braced against the door, having a hard time staying there, since it was on the high side. I could see why she'd given up the porthole; it was showing nothing but water and shiny bubbles rushing past. The floor had a slant of about forty-five degrees. Things were getting pretty noisy. You'd have thought we were about to crack the sound barrier with afterburners blazing, instead of just plowing through the water at a measly fourteen knots—well, call it fifteen now.

Teddy looked at the metal bar in my hand and started to ask something. I waved her aside, and took a look at the door.

"What gives?" I shouted, searching for a point of attack. "Maybe sailboats normally travel on their ears, but isn't our skipper overdoing it a bit?"

"I think she's carrying sail deliberately," Teddy shouted back. "We draw less water well heeled over. We must be getting out of the lee of the island, into the full force of the wind. That means we should be entering the channel soon. *If* she can find it."

"And if she can't," I said, "things will start getting very wet in here, very suddenly? Well, I'm going to try prying this door open a bit. You stick the wrench in the crack I make, to hold it open. Here." I gave her the tool. "If you try to crown me with it, I'll knock you clear across the cabin. That's a promise."

She gave me a breathless little grin. "All right. It's an armistice. Matt!"

"What?"

"There's somebody outside the door, a guard! I just heard him move. A couple of times before I thought I heard something, but—"

I glanced at her, and put my ear to the door. After a moment, I heard him, too, quite plainly, as he struck a match, presumably lighting a cigarette. I wondered how long he'd been standing out there, and how much he'd heard. Not much, with the noise the ship was making. If he'd heard me working in the bathroom, he'd have come in to investigate.

However, we certainly weren't going to break the door down with him standing there. I thought for a moment, and went quickly back into the head and opened every valve in sight. At first I thought it wasn't going to work, although we were on the low side of the ship. Then water rose in the toilet bowl and started sloshing over with the schooner's motion. It ran across the floor and into the cabin as the *Freya* rolled. I beckoned the kid to me, and told her what to do.

"If it's Nick, he won't fall for it," she protested. "He knows the ship is sound."

"It won't be Nick," I said, hoping I was right. "Big Nick's needed on deck at a time like this. It'll be landlubber Loeffler or his unseen pal. Go on."

I stationed myself in the cabin, slipping the iron bar behind the edge of the bunk. Teddy glanced at me. I nodded. She stepped forward and hammered on the door with her small fists.

"Help!" she shouted. "Help, we're going to drown! The water's coming in. Oh, help us, please!"

It was pretty corny. For a moment, there was no response. Then somebody fumbled with the bolt. I didn't recognize his voice.

"Get back. Don't try anything funny."

The door swung open, slamming hard against the dresser. A big man with a pug's thick ears and flattened nose appeared, hanging onto both doorjambs to keep himself from being pitched into the slanting cabin by the force of gravity. He looked at me, safely out of the way, and at the kid.

"There!" she cried, pointing to the water on the floor. "It's coming in, more all the time! We've tried to stop it, but nothing helps!"

He was a landlubber, too. He didn't like the idea of a ship springing a leak, even a little one, with him on board. He took a step forward, still holding the edge of the door with one hand, swinging towards the bathroom. As he turned away from me briefly, I picked up the iron bar and smashed it across his kidneys. He came erect and more than erect. He bent backwards like a bow, grabbing himself back there; then he doubled over with a gasping moan.

I put him down for good with a crack across the neck, and went on my knees to search him for a gun, although if he'd had one, he'd presumably have had it ready when he came in. But I just wasn't passing up any more bets of that kind. But he was clean. He was strictly muscle, the jailer type; and jailers don't carry guns for prisoners to take away from them. Loeffler would supply the brains and artillery for the combination. Well, if he'd had a gun, he'd have been harder to take; we couldn't have it both ways.

I rose. Teddy was staring at the dead man, wide-eyed, her hand to her mouth. I said irritably, "What the hell did you think I was going to do, spend half an hour tearing sheets into strips so I could bind and gag him, like in the movies?"

She drew a deep, ragged breath. "All right. I—I'm all right. What—do we do now?"

"How many ways are there of getting up on deck—"

As I said it, the *Freya* struck. There was no mistaking it this time. She hit hard enough to throw us both to the end of the cabin. There was a sickening moment of scraping and grinding, and she came free, gathering speed again, but the water outside the porthole seemed to have changed color. Maybe it was my imagination, but it seemed to have turned brownish with roiled-up mud or sand.

"There must have been a bar across the mouth of the channel." Teddy's voice was husky. She cleared her throat and spoke breathlessly. "There are three hatches. One leads from the owner's cabin directly into the cockpit. One opens on deck from the main cabin—"

"I know that one. Just back of the mainmast."

"—and there's a scuttle way up forward, with a ladder from the foc's'le."

"Scuttle," I said. "I'll take the scuttle, whatever it may be. We'll use Louis' plan with a change of cast. You get back there where you can watch the cockpit and Mrs. Rosten. Don't let her see you. I'll start some action up forward. When you see a chance, when she's distracted, get that shotgun away from her. I don't mind pistols so much, nobody's going to hit anything with a pistol on a boat jumping around like this, but buckshot scares me. She'll have her hands full, steering. You get the gun. Don't try to use it if you don't know how; just pitch it overboard. Okay?"

"Okay," she breathed. "Matt?"

"Yes, kid?"

She paused in the doorway, and glanced at her father. "If I was wrong—if I was wrong, I apologize."

I stood there for a moment after she'd gone down the passage. Then made a face at my own thoughts, and hauled myself out of there. With my impromptu weapon in my hand, I made my way forward, through a kitchen or galley, into a wedge-shaped compartment that held two bunks, another seagoing john, a washbasin, and an iron ladder leading up into a kind of miniature deckhouse with a curved, slanting roof, half of which slid on tracks. I took a chance on being seen, shoved the lid forward, and got a faceful of spray. I elbowed myself up and out and found myself on the pointed, tilting, streaming deck forward of the masts.

I looked around for Nick and couldn't see him. The long bowsprit was empty. So much for clairvoyance.

It looked as if I'd damn well better see the coach after the game and turn in my crystal ball. Loeffler wasn't in sight, either. From where I clung, I couldn't see the cockpit for masts and sails and rigging. I started to crawl to windward for a better viewpoint, and stopped, looking around, aghast. Until that moment, I hadn't really noticed what we were sailing through.

I mean, it wasn't just that the damn sea was going crazy all around us; I'd kind of expected that. Way off to port and behind us I thought I saw a shadow that could have been Mendenhall Island; way off to starboard I thought I saw the loom of the land. The rest was just broken water, with the spray ripped off the crests of the waves by the howling wind. All right, I'd seen that before; but the thing that really shook me was that the damn stuff was *glowing*.

I'm not kidding. Ask anybody who knows the Bay. Call it phosphorescence, call it what you like: those waves lit up like neon tubes when they broke. The stuff that washed aboard as the schooner put her lee rail under shone pale whitish green; and all around us the foam was luminous. A man with a literary turn of mind might have said we were sailing through the coldly burning seas of hell...

He almost got me while I crouched there, staring. I didn't hear him, of course. Up there, you couldn't hear anything except the cracking roar that was the *Freya's* bow splitting the water. I just felt him, I guess. I knew it was time to move by the instinct you get after long years of this work; and I threw myself aside as he dropped out of the rigging. He landed where I'd been. I caught a fistful of ropes on the foremast and cut at him with the johnny-lever and hit nothing but solid shoulder muscle. The bar just bounced.

He came for me, his white teeth shining in his black face. He seemed to be made of the same kind of crazy, luminous stuff as the sea around us. Just the same, it should have been easy. A good man with a stick ought to be able to handle a fair-sized mob or a full-grown male gorilla. I was pretty good at fencing long before anybody in this country ever heard of *kindo*. I should have been able to pick his eyes out of his head, smash his Adam's apple, and tear his guts out. No matter how big he was. I should have been able to take him easily, and I could have, too, if the damn ship had only stood still.

It didn't seem to bother him. His bare feet seemed to cling to the slanting deck. I feinted at his head as he moved in. He ducked, throwing up an arm, wide open. Still clinging to the mast, I gave him the end of the bar in the stomach, as hard as I could from that position.

It wasn't hard enough. He was made of tarred rope and old whalebone. It stopped him momentarily, but I was clumsy recovering. There was supposed to be some fancy footwork in here, but I was having a hard enough time just staying on the boat. I chopped at his head and got a forearm instead, not hard enough; then he had me by the arm. I remembered what had happened to Louis' arm under similar circumstances. Well, it had been a loused-up operation from the very beginning...

The *Freya* hit bottom, hard. It made him lose his grip and hurled him forward, away from me. I went to my knees, still clinging to my friendly halyards, if that's what they were; but he was lying there in the bow, momentarily dazed, and I let go and went after him. The schooner hit again, throwing me off balance, and bumped along the bottom, losing speed. A big wave broke over the rail and sent solid water sluicing across the deck.

"*Nick!*" It was Robin Rosten's voice, sounding miles away. "*Nick, damn you, call it! Give me the course!*"

Nick picked himself up, jumped over me, and reached the foremast in three bounds. He ran right up it, using the wooden hoops of the foresail as a ladder. I saw him take one look around up there.

"*Bear off, ma'am. Helm a'weather…*"

The schooner swung to leeward. For a moment I wouldn't have put money on it either way; then, slowly, the bottom lost its grip on the keel and we began to gain speed again.

"*Steady as you go!*"

He was still up there, calling it. What he could see ahead of us, I didn't know. It all looked like the same phosphorescent welter of spray and foam to me. It was, I thought, a hell of a place for an innocent boy from the arid state of New Mexico; but while he was up the mast, I'd better attend to business aft.

"*Look sharp on deck! Prisoner loose!*"

His bellow alerted them before I got amidships. I saw Loeffler's head appear above the deckhouse. There was a little spit of flame, but I'd anticipated that and thrown myself down. I don't know where the bullet went. I crawled after with my iron bar, wondering how to get at him without getting shot.

"Luff her, ma'am! Luff her hard!"

That was Big Nick up in the crosstrees, conning the ship. I didn't have to worry about him for a while... Suddenly the schooner was coming upright; the deck was level under my feet; and all the sails were breaking into thunderous flapping as the ship ran up into the wind. He must have slid down a rope somehow, because there he was, riding the boom of the foresail in. He launched himself at me from the spar, bellowing something to his mistress at the wheel. It was kind of like playing tag with Tarzan of the apes.

It was too bad, really. I mean, he'd given it a good try. You had to give him A for effort. He'd just made one mistake; he'd given me, for a moment, a level deck to fight on. I wasn't where he landed; and when he reached for me, I was set. The *kindo* rule is: thrust to the soft, cut to the hard. I didn't take a chance on going in close for a quick finish. I just swung with all my strength and broke the hard bone of his arm between wrist and elbow.

Then the sails were filling again, the *Freya* was heeling over, water was coming over the rail, and Big Nick tried to grab at the mainmast to catch himself, but that was the arm that no longer worked. He went down into the torrent pouring along the deck to leeward, and was washed aft. I went after him, but ducked as Loeffler thrust his head and

gun out of the cockpit. The bullet dug splinters out of the
deck to my left.

"Don't you shoot him, man! He's mine!"

That was Nick, picking himself out of the scuppers.
Loeffler was taking aim for a second shot. Nick knocked
him cockeyed. I saw the pistol glint in the air, flying out
to sea. Nick was coming forward past the deckhouse.
Behind him, I saw Loeffler painfully pull himself up and
crawl towards something in the cockpit: the shotgun.

Whether he was planning to use it on Nick or me will
never be known, because as he turned, a small figure
jumped him from nowhere and twisted the gun in his
hands. Mr. Loeffler must already have had the safety off
and his finger on the trigger. The twelve-gauge fired and
blew off most of his head. Even in the darkness, he was
a fairly horrible sight, as he toppled over backwards into
the glowing wake.

Big Nick had paid attention to none of this. He'd been
stalking me slowly, but I wasn't worried about a one-armed
man, no matter how big and tough. I waited for him, braced
against a skylight amidships. When he rushed, I again gave
him the feint to the head that brought his good arm up.
Then I stepped in with the steel bar held low in both hands
and all my weight behind it, driving it in hard from below,
up under the ribs to rupture the diaphragm…

When I got back into the cockpit, Teddy had Robin
Rosten covered with the shotgun. The kid looked very
small in her drenched romper suit—nobody was staying
dry on deck tonight—and her face was white and sick.

"I—I can't!" she gasped. "I ought to shoot her, but I can't!"

"Sure," I said. I took the gun from her, dropping the bar.

"That man!" she wailed. "I didn't mean to—it just went off! Did you see—"

I put my left arm around her to steady her. "Hell, that's nothing," I said. "I saw a guy with two heads once. In a bottle in the Smithsonian."

She stared at me with complete horror; then she giggled hysterically and pressed her face against my jacket. I looked at Robin. She was soaked like the rest of us, her jeans and sweater glistening wet. Her gaudy kerchief was gone, and the long dark hair had blown loose and was streaming out to leeward. She was using all her strength on the big steering wheel as the schooner plunged ahead. Behind her, the wake ran back into the darkness. Way back there, I saw spray flash up white; there was a boat chasing us, as we'd guessed, below.

"That's about it, lady," I said. "Let's bring this seagoing trolley to a halt, huh?"

She looked at me for a moment, ignoring the shotgun tucked under my arm. She glanced back over her shoulder briefly, and faced me again. She smiled slowly.

"Very well," she said. "If you say so, Mr. Helm."

She turned and hauled at the wheel, using her foot in the lower spokes for leverage. I felt Teddy look up. The schooner seemed to rise as the wind came aft. The wheel was spinning more easily now. Robin looked at me and laughed as I brought the shotgun up.

"Go ahead," she called. "Shoot. Get blood all over the deck."

She glanced up at the towering triangle of mainsail above us. I followed the direction of her look and saw the taut canvas slacken and curl oddly as the wind got behind it. If there had ever been a time to shoot, it was too late now. The great main boom began to swing...

I threw myself down into the cockpit, carrying the kid with me. Robin stood firmly braced against the wheel, still laughing. Up forward, the two other sails came over with a crash, shaking the ship. One must have split, because canvas started flapping. The mainsail gathered momentum quite slowly, it seemed. As the great timber swung past over our heads, Robin Rosten stepped up on the cockpit coaming and went over the side in a clean dive.

The schooner went clear over on her side as the mainsail slammed across; then she hit the shoals and the masts came down.

23

I flew over the spot in a Navy plane the following afternoon. The schooner was still lying there, half awash. I could have told them it wasn't going anywhere. You get that much boat crosswise in a narrow channel in shallow water, and where's it going to go? It can't even sink very far. It wasn't as if we'd hit a coral reef with a hundred fathoms on either side.

I'd tried to tell them that the night before, but communications had been poor in the storm, and they'd insisted on rescuing us, which was why I was taped up like a mummy, having broken two ribs in the process. At that, I was lucky not to have lost a leg in somebody's propellers while being hauled to safety, as they laughingly called it, at the end of a rope. It had been a hell of a wet and heroic business. If they'd just waited until the wind dropped the following morning, they could have taken us off dryshod in a birchbark canoe.

We flew on down the Bay and out to sea. Now that

the weather was clearing, we were looking for a freighter. We found three of them, all claiming perfectly legitimate business in the area. Two of them were probably telling the truth. Maybe all three of them were. We radioed Washington and were told to forget it and come home; they'd handle it some other way. After dinner, I went to see Louis in the hospital. He looked like an Egyptian mummy.

"Have they found her yet?" he whispered.

"No," I said. "No, there's been no sign of her."

"They won't find her," he whispered—and they never did. If she drowned, she never came up. I don't think she drowned. Some people don't drown easy.

Leaving there, I saw Teddy and young Orcutt sitting in the lobby, holding hands. He was the hero of the occasion, of course. It was he who, looking for Teddy, had come to the Rosten place and found everybody missing. He'd sighted the schooner heading down the Bay and, on a hunch, had run down to the dock, wound up the power cruiser *Osprey*, and taken off after us. He'd trailed us back in the mist all day, closing in after dark. When he saw us heading into the prohibited area, he'd got on the cruiser's marine radio and called for official help. He was also the boy who'd swum a rope over to us after we'd piled up, and helped Teddy across to the rescue vessel.

The kid looked very cute and demure in a pink cotton dress carefully arranged to display some pretty petticoat ruffles as she sat. They were grateful for everything I'd done, she said. Her eyes were uneasy. Obviously she wasn't quite sure about me, one way or another. It was like waking from a nightmare, and the details were a little blurred, but she certainly didn't want to be reminded of anything she'd promised or implied under strain, like demonstrating her gratitude in a practical way. Orcutt said he was very grateful, too.

Mac was behind his desk when I came into the office. He looked up, waved me to a chair, and said, "Haakonsen, Ivar. Half-Danish, half-Russian. Not strictly in our line of work, but versatile. We first came across him in fifty-four. A second-stringer, but moving up."

"I couldn't recall his name," I said. "I knew it wasn't Loeffler."

"The other one went by the name of Mike Hamisky. Ex-boxer, considered a little punchy. We've turned up nothing derogatory so far. We're still checking."

"Sure," I said.

"As for Louis Rosten, we'll do what we can, in view of what you report."

"Sure."

"I am instructed to commend you for a very satisfactory job. The other solution would have been acceptable, but this one, since it worked, makes everybody much happier."

"Sure," I said. "Naturally I had that in mind all along, sir. You know I just love to make people happy."

"I know," he said. "That is your most endearing trait, I think, Eric. Aside from your great respect for discipline and instant obedience to orders, I mean."

"Yes, sir," I said.

He looked at me for a moment across the big desk. He said gently, "You lucked out, didn't you?"

I said, "Yes. It was a mess from start to finish, but I lucked out at the end."

"It happens like that," he said. "But it's not something an agent can count on."

"No, sir," I said. "That's why I'm submitting my resignation, sir."

He didn't move. After a moment, he said, rather impatiently, "Don't be melodramatic. When I want your resignation, I'll ask for it, never fear." I didn't say anything. After a moment, he reached into the top desk drawer and pulled out an official-looking folder. He glanced at it, and slid it across the desk to me. "Read that before you do anything hasty."

I looked at the folder. The neatly typed label read: ELLINGTON, MRS. LAURA H. *Autopsy Report Cop. 3*. I couldn't remember any Mrs. Ellington. Then I remembered that Jean had used that name.

"Go on," Mac said. "Read it."

I said, "It will be three pages of medical jargon. You tell me what it says."

"It says you didn't kill her."

I looked at him. "If I didn't, who did?"

"She did."

"Come again."

"She drank herself to death."

I grimaced. "That's ridiculous, sir. You don't die of cirrhosis in the time she'd been at it, and it doesn't hit you like that, anyway. Who's kidding whom?"

"I didn't say anything about cirrhosis. Did Jean down a stiff drink—six or eight ounces of straight whisky, say—a few minutes before she died? The autopsy says she did."

I said, "Sure, but—"

"It killed her," he said. "Don't look so surprised. It happens all the time, young people showing off how much they can drink right out of the bottle, and falling over dead. That much alcohol in one dose can be pure poison under certain circumstances. The heart just stops."

"I see," I said slowly. "I see."

"According to your own report, you made several mistakes during the past few days. But that is one you did not make. Your hand did not slip. Under the circumstances, do you wish to reconsider the resignation you haven't turned in yet?"

I hesitated. I'd come in with my mind made up, I thought; and there was really no reason why this should change things in any way, but somehow it did.

Mac's voice came to me gently, "Perhaps you'd like to take the month that is coming to you and think it over. On medical recommendations, I could make that a little longer."

"A month should do it," I said.

As I said it, I tried to remember what I'd been going to do with a month's leave. I'd had something in mind, a long time ago. Well, it would come back to me as soon as I got some sleep. If it didn't, it couldn't be very important.

"Oh, Eric," he said, as I rose and turned towards the

door. I looked back. "Try the Presidential Hotel, Room 212. The lady didn't leave her name, but she had our number, so she must have worked for us once. The girl who took the call said the accent was from Texas."

I stood there for a moment. Then I said, "Thank you, sir," and moved quickly towards the door.

"Eric."

"Yes, sir?"

"I still don't approve," he said, but he didn't say it very severely.

ABOUT THE AUTHOR

Donald Hamilton was the creator of secret agent Matt Helm, star of 27 novels that have sold more than 20 million copies worldwide.

Born in Sweden, he emigrated to the United States and studied at the University of Chicago. During the Second World War he served in the United States Naval Reserve, and in 1941 he married Kathleen Stick, with whom he had four children.

The first Matt Helm book, *Death of a Citizen*, was published in 1960 to great acclaim, and four of the subsequent novels were made into motion pictures starring Dean Martin in the title role. A new Matt Helm movie is currently in pre-production at Steven Spielberg's Dreamworks studio. Hamilton was also the author of several outstanding stand-alone thrillers and westerns, including two novels adapted for the big screen as *The Big Country* and *The Violent Men*.

Donald Hamilton died in 2006.

COMING SOON FROM TITAN BOOKS

PRAISE FOR DONALD HAMILTON

"Donald Hamilton has brought to the spy novel
the authentic hard realism of Dashiell Hammett;
and his stories are as compelling, and probably
as close to the sordid truth of espionage,
as any now being told."
Anthony Boucher, *The New York Times*

"This series by Donald Hamilton is the top-ranking
American secret agent fare, with its intelligent
protagonist and an author who consistently writes
in high style. Good writing, slick plotting and
stimulating characters, all tartly flavored with wit."
Book Week

"Matt Helm is as credible a man of violence as has
ever figured in the fiction of intrigue."
The New York Sunday Times

"Fast, tightly written, brutal, and very good…"
Milwaukee Journal

TITANBOOKS.COM

The Man From Hell
by Barrie Roberts

Séance For A Vampire
by Fred Saberhagen

The Seventh Bullet
by Daniel D. Victor

The Whitechapel Horrors
by Edward B. Hanna

Dr. Jekyll and Mr. Holmes
by Loren D. Estleman

The Angel of the Opera
by Sam Siciliano

The Giant Rat of Sumatra
by Richard L. Boyer

The Peerless Peer
by Philip José Farmer

The Star of India
by Carole Buggé

TITANBOOKS.COM

COMING IN 2014 FROM TITAN BOOKS

King of the Weeds

BY MICKEY SPILLANE & MAX ALLAN COLLINS

THE PENULTIMATE MIKE HAMMER NOVEL

As his old friend Captain Pat Chambers of Homicide approaches retirement, Hammer finds himself up against a clever serial killer targeting only cops.

A killer Chambers had put away many years ago is suddenly freed on new, apparently indisputable evidence, and Hammer wonders if, somehow, this seemingly placid, very odd old man might be engineering cop killings that all seem to be either accidental or by natural causes.

At the same time Hammer and Velda are dealing with the fallout—some of it mob, some of it federal government—over the $89 billion dollar cache the detective is (rightly) suspected of finding not long ago…

TITANBOOKS.COM